A frisson of danger sparked in the stormy atmosphere.

But then Leo almost smiled. "I don't want to argue with you."

"No?" Rosanna couldn't take her gaze off him. "You just want everything your own way." She stood up from the stool. "I'm not marrying you. Ever."

"Why not give us a chance?" He, too, stood and walked around the counter.

"There is no us," she muttered. "There's just a... situation."

"But there could be." He advanced closer, and the glint in his eyes froze her. "*You're* the one not thinking creatively now."

She couldn't think at all anymore. Not when he was this near, this intense, this determined.

"Why can't we make it what *we* want?" he asked softly.

Want?

Rosanna couldn't breathe. There was lightning now—fully charged attraction that was impossible to deny yet almost too much to bear. All because he'd come to stand right before her. Of all the people in the world, why did her body want him? A man who was bossy and authoritative and serious? Why this unemotional, ruthless, unforgiving man? Yet she'd just sparked to life.

Rebels, Brothers, Billionaires

Reputation precedes them, temptation will redeem them.

Playboy Ash and hard-edged Leo Castle are just two of their philandering father's heirs. Which means they've inherited much more than a huge fortune and luxury property portfolio. Their father's notoriety follows them wherever they go...

Determined to step out of the shadow of scandal, the half brothers strive to defy expectation at every turn. Until rebellion comes up against desire so strong it's halted in its tracks!

Discover Ash's story in
Stranded for One Scandalous Week

And read Leo's story in
Nine Months to Claim Her

Both available now!

Natalie Anderson

NINE MONTHS TO CLAIM HER

HARLEQUIN® PRESENTS®

Recycling programs for this product may not exist in your area.

ISBN-13: 978-1-335-56778-9

Nine Months to Claim Her

Copyright © 2021 by Natalie Anderson

This edition published by arrangement with Harlequin Books S.A.

For questions and comments about the quality of this book, please contact us at CustomerService@Harlequin.com.

Harlequin Enterprises ULC
22 Adelaide St. West, 40th Floor
Toronto, Ontario M5H 4E3, Canada
www.Harlequin.com

Printed in U.S.A.

USA TODAY bestselling author **Natalie Anderson** writes emotional contemporary romance full of sparkling banter, sizzling heat and uplifting endings—perfect for readers who love to escape with empowered heroines and arrogant alphas who are too sexy for their own good. When she's not writing, you'll find Natalie wrangling her four children, three cats, two goldfish and one dog... and snuggled in a heap on the sofa with her husband at the end of the day. Follow her at natalie-anderson.com.

Books by Natalie Anderson

Harlequin Presents

Awakening His Innocent Cinderella
Pregnant by the Commanding Greek
The Greek's One-Night Heir
Secrets Made in Paradise

Conveniently Wed!

The Innocent's Emergency Wedding

Once Upon a Temptation

Shy Queen in the Royal Spotlight

Rebels, Brothers, Billionaires

Stranded for One Scandalous Week

The Christmas Princess Swap

The Queen's Impossible Boss

Visit the Author Profile page
at Harlequin.com for more titles.

For Jo,

Thank you so much for our weekend escape
to the seaside and time to stare at pretty cows!
LOL. I so appreciate your friendship and support.
Here's to some more fabulous time away writing.

CHAPTER ONE

'Rose Gold? It's been for ever!'

Rosanna Gold smiled through gritted teeth, inwardly groaning—yet again—that her parents had thought it clever and cute to name her Rose. It had even been part of their marketing plan for when she took over the family business from her father Red. But it wasn't clever or cute. It was cringeworthy, even more so given she was never going to take over the company. When she was introduced, people invariably giggled then commented on the fact that her hair was far more carrot than rose gold. She'd heard the same jokes a million times and when she'd finally moved out she'd lengthened her name to Rosanna. But tonight, she was back home. Back to being 'Rose'. Back to trying to please her parents. Back to being less than either the beauty or treasure her name suggested.

And it turned out that the opening celebration of the latest luxury apartment complex in central Sydney, built by property conglomerate Castle Holdings, was basically a horror of a high-school reunion: 'Ten Years On'—and it was still terrible.

'Mae, how lovely to see you.' Rosanna hoped her inevitable blush would recede quickly—she'd been flushing stop-sign-red all night.

Born and bred Sydney society elite, Mae Wilson had been in the year below Rosanna at school, but she'd always been decades ahead in style. So, of course, she was one of the well-heeled new residents of Kingston Towers. Only the absolute cream of Sydney society could afford one of the ultra-stylish inner-city apartments with their sleek security systems and every convenience imaginable.

'What brings you here tonight?' Mae asked.

The surprise in Mae's tone, and the mere fact that she'd even asked, hammered it home. Rosanna didn't belong in Kingston Towers. She probably would never have set foot in the place had her mother not begged.

She'd been woken early this morning by an awful call informing her that her parents had been in a car accident and she was needed in Sydney urgently. Freaked out, she'd raced from her town a few hours north, panicking the whole way. Only when she'd arrived at the hospital it was to discover she wasn't there for a bedside vigil. While her father would be in plaster for the next few weeks, he would recover fully, and fortunately her mother had only bruises… No, it turned out their 'SOS' summons had been about this *party* and how crucial it was that a Gold family member attended. And the only one able to go now was Rosanna.

Her initial relief that they weren't badly hurt had been washed over by the old frustration of past years. She shouldn't have been surprised. Her parents' business had always been the priority in their lives—coming ahead of everything and everyone else, even themselves and their *own* well-being and certainly Rosanna's as well. She'd tried to convince her mother that one party didn't matter. But, apparently, it did.

'My parents did the fit-out of some of the lounge spaces.' Rosanna maintained her smile.

For the last two decades her parents' company, Gold Style, had done the interior design for Castle Holdings properties. But when Hugh Castle had died a year ago things had changed. While they'd all expected Ash, Hugh's legitimate—albeit wayward—heir to assume control, it had been Leo Castle, Hugh's illegitimate son, who'd taken over as CEO of the conglomerate. It had been a shock, given Hugh had refused to recognise Leo right till the end. The shocks had kept coming since. A 'control freak' was how Rosanna's mother had described Leo this morning. A 'workaholic' who already headed another business in insurance and now ruled Castle Holdings with an iron fist and an acute eye. Apparently he was fiercely driven and uncompromising and in her parents' view that *wasn't* a good thing. Because he'd put Castle Holdings' interiors contracts out to tender, inviting proposals from her parents' competitors. Gold Style would no longer automatically secure them—and hadn't, in fact.

'Oh, Gold Style.' Mae nodded dismissively. 'Of course, I'd forgotten you were connected to them.'

Not just connected, she was their *daughter*. Their only child. And honestly? Their greatest disappointment.

'Wear that navy empire line dress,' her mother had shrilly instructed in amongst her barrage of information this morning. 'It's more flattering.'

Because Rosanna's body *needed* flattering—as always her pale freckled skin and uneven posture needed to be concealed. Appearances mattered to maintain and build the success of the business and imperfections were not allowed—not speckled skin, or a spine so curved by scoliosis that not even surgery could properly straighten it, at least not to the point of pleasing her perfectionist parents. But while Rosanna had obeyed the instruction to attend the party, she hadn't been able to wear that particular dress. She'd had only a few things at her parents' apartment and had opted for a silk black blouse and skirt. Her mother had always preferred Rosanna didn't wear skirts because the hemlines reflected the unevenness of her waist, but this one was long and hopefully that slight tilt on one side wasn't noticeable. But even though her outfit fulfilled the covering-up element, it wasn't really good enough for Kingston Towers society.

She'd let her parents down again and that hurt. That her mother had even *asked* had made her want to succeed just this *once* for them. Of course she'd yes, even though parties this fancy, in places this elite, weren't her forte. She'd always felt shy and awkward. But this morning her mother had been more upset than Rosanna had ever seen her. She knew their company was everything, but she'd wondered if the accident had shaken her mother more than she was admitting. She'd repeatedly insisted that Rosanna attend—someone from the Gold family needed to be 'seen' by the CEO himself.

But two hours in and Rosanna had yet to meet Leo Castle. It was her own fault, given she didn't even know what he looked like. She didn't bother much with Sydney society nor with social media either. However, she *had* briefly seen Leo's half-brother, Ash Castle—the 'legitimate' heir who'd rebelled and refused to have anything to do with his late father's company. That Ash had even been here tonight was a surprise because he'd avoided anything related to Hugh Castle for years. He must have a better relationship with his half-brother than he'd ever had with his father. Even so, Rosanna hadn't had the confidence to ask Ash to introduce her to Leo because unfortunately Ash Castle was the source of Rosanna's most mortifying teen moment. While it had been public humiliation of the online kind—and the reason she preferred to live a social-media-free life—the worst had been her parents' reaction. They'd placed the blame squarely on Rosanna's uneven shoulders and the impact of their displeasure still weighed on her today. That was why she was here now—still trying to please them for once.

But while Ash had been unusually quiet and courteous, it had been yet another awkward high-school reunion—especially when he'd briefly brought up that cringe thing in their past. She'd only got through it because she'd realised just what hell he'd have been under at the time. But maybe the fact that she'd spoken to *him* for the first time in a decade would suffice for her parents' expectations for the evening? He was a Castle, after all.

'I heard something about you being a university professor now,' Mae said, drawing her attention back to the present. 'You always were a brain box.'

Rosanna inwardly groaned again at her parents' inflated description of her job. When reality wasn't good enough, they embellished—always over the top. In fact she was a laboratory technician at the school of Biological Sciences at East River University, a couple of hours north of Sydney. As for being a brain box? That was only because she'd spent her life working insanely hard to maintain the grades that were the one thing her parents seemed to be proud of her for. Not that it had ever garnered her any social currency—Mae was one of those people who'd only ever spoken to Rosanna when she'd wanted to borrow her study notes.

'Not a professor.' She smiled resolutely. 'I take some lectures.'

Even that was a stretch. She tutored first-year science students because, according to her boss, she was 'good at instilling scrupulous understanding of the scientific method'. But the work had become repetitive and frustrating. Yet again she'd not lived up to expectations because she should, at the very least, be a full-time lecturer by now if only she'd lived up to her 'potential'.

And as she determinedly chatted with Mae, her energy wilted.

'I'm sorry, I've just got to go and talk to…' Rosanna glanced around the room, hoping to spot someone—*anyone* '… Harry.'

Her excuse to end the current conversation worked again. It had been working well all evening.

Breathing out, Rosanna walked away from the other guests, wondering whether it was too soon to sneak away or if she ought to 'fly the family flag' a little longer.

It had been a failed mission from the beginning. She knew her glamorous, party-professional parents had been disappointed in her reserved nature as a child, in her increasingly flawed appearance. They'd been disappointed by her decision not to stay in Sydney and follow them into the family business after 'all they'd done', and they'd *definitely* been disappointed by her inability to secure a society son-in-law of their dreams to lift their profile all the more…

But the fact was, Rosanna had never satisfied *anyone's* dreams. Not even her own.

She laughed beneath her breath at her self-piteous moment. She'd been so busy trying to meet the impossible dreams of her parents she'd not stopped to actually dream any of her own. And now? Now she had no clue what it was *she* wanted.

But Kingston Towers? The whole complex was dreamy. The party was on the penultimate level of the East Tower with stunning views across the city and to the second, slightly taller tower. She'd toured the two apartments open for viewing already, but from here she could glimpse the West Tower penthouse. Was that a hint of a terraced garden? Her curiosity was piqued and temptation stirred. Rosanna couldn't resist a garden. And it was a showing, after all. Given she was unlikely to ever get the opportunity again, she walked to the central elevators—taking a moment from the horrible party for herself. One elevator opened the second she summoned it and inside she pressed the very top button.

Moments later she arrived at the penthouse. She stepped out, savouring the silence and the sensation of *escape*. The tranquillity was a welcome contrast to the heavy bass downstairs and the hum of people loudly talking to counter it. The other guests couldn't yet have realised they could inspect this apartment as well.

Rosanna was glad to explore it alone. No more awkward reunions for just a minute.

The glass doors leading out to the terrace were thrown wide open in invitation, so what else was to be done? Outside she breathed deeply, appreciating the scent of summer and the warm breeze. As she'd suspected, the terrace garden was a gorgeous space brimming with verdant vitality. There were cleverly placed trellises covered with foliage and structural plants that provided privacy and shelter around a comfortable seating area. In an instant she felt better. With all the greenery she could almost forget she was in the middle of a large city. Though if she glanced beyond the leaf-woven trellis, the view of the gleaming harbour was incredible. But it was the garden that truly entranced her.

As she explored the deceptively large space the sky began to turn. Small lights hidden amongst the foliage automatically beamed on. It softened the atmosphere and made it even more intimate. To her wonderment, tucked away on the other side of the trellis was a small pool. She knew there was a lane pool on the recreation level for the residents but this was smaller, a place to plunge rather than exhaust oneself with endless laps. The surrounding plants were flowering and had luscious deep green leaves and with the lights it made the place feel like a magical den. A sensation of peace and pleasure washed over her as one plant in particular caught her eye with its contrasting green foliage.

She'd found not just a sanctuary, but a *paradise*.

Leo Castle sprawled in the large chair in the study, silently watching the uninvited woman wander around his private terrace. She wasn't supposed to be here. Then again, nor was he. He was supposed to be downstairs talking with the new and prospective owners of the luxury apartments Castle Holdings had just completed. Socialising was his most loathed business task—mainly because it interrupted the actual business of doing business. His phone had been humming in his pocket when he was talking to guests downstairs, vibrating with notification after notification. In the end he couldn't resist stealing up here to check in because his favourite aspect was the deal—sale and purchase, the constant accumulation of security. He liked to work fast, accurately, viciously, relentlessly. So missing messages when he had a new deal on a knife-edge was not his idea of fun. But since he'd come up here he'd more than caught up. The outstanding deal had just come through. In theory he should now go down and celebrate the lot. In theory he should be the happiest he'd ever been. Because in theory, he finally had everything he'd ever wanted.

For almost thirty years—his entire life—he'd fought to get to this position. Fighting for recognition, for *justice*...for everything that had been denied him for so long. His name and honour, respect and reputation, fortune...all were finally fully within his control. And nothing mattered to him more than having complete control over his own damned destiny.

Kingston Towers—his first major project as the new CEO of Castle Holdings—was an undeniable success. The man who'd built the company from the ground up, Hugh Castle, had died a year ago. Leo had taken over from the man who'd not only refused to acknowledge Leo's existence, but done everything possible to deny him his rights. But Leo had no intention of letting that happen for ever. He'd talked to his half-brother, Ash, the 'rightful' heir. Ash hadn't wanted anything to do with their father's business—he'd have been happy to see it burn. But Leo had been determined to make the company what it *should* have been and so he and Ash had agreed he'd take the reins. In this last year he'd carved out the cronyism, the favours, the hidden deceitful deals—battling the resentment of the old guard wanting to hold on to their unearned privileges and the pressure to prove himself worthy when he'd been unrecognised for so long. But he'd accomplished what he'd wanted—all while maintaining the success of his own company that he'd built simply to prove he could. He'd worked every minute he'd been awake for *years* to get here. Hours of stress and toil and sacrifice. And he'd done it. He'd even claimed this jewel at the top of the tower for himself. Yet now he was here he didn't feel any real satisfaction. He felt…*nothing.*

Well, not *nothing.*

Because there was—as always—that acidic burning regret in the pit of his stomach that his mother wasn't alive to see any of it. She was never to know *her* honour had been restored, never to feel any peace or security or enjoyment of the rewards…which meant that he couldn't either. Because it was *his* fault she couldn't. Leo rolled his shoulders, unable to dwell on that most painful of wounds.

Maybe he was tired, but he didn't want to return to his duty downstairs yet. And he didn't have to, right? Because Ash had made an appearance. Ash, who'd tracked Leo down when they were both angry teens.

Rebellious Ash, who'd enabled Leo to prove their shared parentage. Ash, who'd stepped aside and been an ally ever since.

Leo would always owe him. But their bond was built on more than mutual loathing of their father now. There was respect and loyalty. Ash had signalled his support of Leo's leadership of the company and Leo had done all he could to support Ash's fiercely independent business in return. It was the one relationship in Leo's life now that actually worked and Ash was the only family Leo would ever have. Leo hadn't failed to notice how haunted he'd looked earlier today. He suspected there might be a woman involved but he'd not asked. He'd have been unable to offer any advice anyway; it was for Ash to work out alone. But for now Ash was downstairs doing what he did best—avoiding whatever it was causing him grief by outrageously charming everyone he encountered.

Which meant Leo didn't have to. Leo didn't have to even *be* 'Leo Castle', right now. He could just be a man watching a mysterious, pretty woman out on the terrace.

The elevator had chimed its low warning a few moments ago. He'd neglected to lock it again when he'd come up, but now he swiped through a couple of screens on his phone, adjusting settings so the elevator couldn't come back to this floor unless summoned by him. No more intruders today. No one but the female currently prowling through his plants.

He didn't think she was a guest. Clad in a black blouse and black skirt and black heels that were more sensible than skyscraper, she was staff, he guessed. A waitress escaping all those trays of hors d'oeuvres for a few minutes. He didn't blame her for wanting some peace, he'd wanted it himself.

He watched her explore the terrace, increasingly fascinated by her unguarded demeanour. She was a slim shadow and even though her hair was tied back he could see it was more flaming orange tones than rich auburn—like bonfire night. Despite the distance and even as the sky turned dusky, he could see her skin was pale. She breathed deeply, taking in the view before turning back to the small garden again. Her hand lightly touched the blooms with a reverence and care that he appreciated. He felt a fleeting desire for her to look up and inspect him with the same deliberate concentration, as if there were nothing and no one else in the world she had any interest in.

Ridiculous.

He half laughed beneath his breath at his fanciful thinking. He *must* be tired. He didn't get distracted. Ever. But with that deal now completed, the party a success, maybe he could have a moment to enjoy the scenery. To stop and smell the roses like his interloper out there...

She cupped one of the flowers with a gentle touch and intense focus. But she didn't pick the bloom. He was glad; he liked those flowers even if they only survived because of the people he paid to take care of them. More importantly, they were his. Not hers. But she suddenly turned to another plant. Her fingers slid across the large, flat leaf and down the stem. A second later she snapped it.

Leo stiffened in incredulity and a second later amusement washed over him.

Little thief.

She'd picked, not a flower, but a stem from an ugly-as-sin plant. Not quite Beauty stealing roses then, and nor was he about to be a Beast and keep her here for his entertainment. But given he'd caught her in the act, he *was* going to call her on it.

'And you are…?'

Rosanna jumped and turned at the low voice. Her reply caught in her throat as she saw him. First impression? Intimidating size. Second? *Eyes.*

They were so blue they were almost indigo and it took only one look at them for her brain to slither into irrelevance and leave her simply staring. Tall, muscular, *magnificent.* He moved towards her slowly, almost carefully, which allowed other details to slowly seep in. His dark suit accentuated his height and the breadth of his shoulders. The man had muscles and he moved with lethal grace, which meant he must use those muscles well and often. His close-cropped hair and chiselled jaw added to his aura of discipline. Adding this to his *very* serious countenance, she guessed he was on the security team. As he moved nearer she saw those blue eyes sharpen, revealing intelligence, alertness and a faint hint of condemnation.

Rosanna was poleaxed. And why on earth was she suddenly thinking a man *magnificent*?

'You know you're not supposed to be here,' he added, overlooking the fact she'd not answered his first question.

'Are you?' she deflected while attempting to catch

both her breath and brain and hoping her flash-flood auto-blush would recede quickly.

'I am.' All authority.

'Security detail?' Catching her breath was impossible. Apparently all the oxygen had been sucked from the world and the plants surrounding her were no help whatsoever.

His shockingly vibrant eyes narrowed. 'You're…on service here?'

Service? She frowned before it dawned. The security guy thought she was a waitress—meaning he had no idea who she was. Rightly so—she really had no influence here, no matter how hard her parents wished it.

'Escaping duty for a little while,' she offered warily. It wasn't a complete lie. 'Besides, won't other—?' She broke off, realising she'd almost given herself away. 'Won't some of the guests be arriving up here shortly?'

His head moved almost imperceptibly. 'No one is supposed to be up here.'

No one? Too late she realised that maybe more people weren't up here because it was supposed to be off-limits.

'Why not?' she asked awkwardly. 'It's the best bit of the whole building.'

There was a hesitation. 'Some of the interior isn't finished so it's not open for a tour tonight.'

'Yet I got up here without any problems.'

'That was a mistake.'

His gaze was so unrelenting she couldn't resist a slight dig.

'Lax security?' she muttered innocently.

'Apparently so,' he acknowledged seriously. 'But I've

locked the elevators now so no one can come up without the code.'

Her breath caught again—he'd *locked* the lift? 'What about getting back down?'

He didn't blink but his mouth twitched almost imperceptibly. Rosanna stared back at him, her own intrigue growing. Had that been a glimmer of *amusement*?

'Are you concerned that you're now stuck up here?' he enquired softly. The edge of tease was so faint. But it was there.

'Not in the least,' she lied, instinctively going for self-preservation.

'Not worried about losing your job?'

'They won't notice for a while.' That wasn't a lie at all.

'I don't believe you,' he said. 'I think the world would notice if you were absent.'

He was *so* far from right but, for just this once, it was nice to go along with it and believe a slightly cheesy line delivered by a sinfully serious man. Her nerves sharpened as awareness shivered along her veins. The sky had darkened further and now they were softly lit by the glow of those small bulbs. It could so easily be mistaken for a fairy den of magic and mystery and enticing amusement… And this flight of flirtish fancy? This ripple of temptation? This was not her. *Ever.*

She didn't think it was him either. But he wasn't moving and nor was she because there was *something* in the air.

She made herself swallow. 'Shouldn't you get back to doing your security rounds?'

'There are plenty of us here. Besides, I'm keeping an eye on you.'

'I'm not about to steal anything.' She half laughed.

'But you already have.' He jerked his chin towards her hand.

'Oh.' She glanced down. She'd forgotten all about the stem of the Monstera plant she'd swiped. Now she realised she was gripping it so tightly it was a wonder she hadn't minced it to pulp. 'That.'

Amusement flickered again, ripping an irreparable tear in his serious facade, and he suddenly smiled—lopsided—as if it was an unfamiliar sensation stretching on his face. 'Yes. That.'

He reached out and took the frond from her and she just let him because now he was smiling. Which meant that now he was spellbinding. Her heart raced in response to his move closer. She was so aware of him that she had to consciously *not* take a step back. It wasn't that he was a danger but that he was a threat of another kind. A threat that was also a temptation. Especially when he smiled.

'Any particular reason for this?' he asked. 'You didn't want a flower?'

'If I picked a flower it would die sooner.'

'So you *care* about the plants?' he mused. 'This wasn't wilful destruction?'

'Of course not.'

His smile deepened as he stepped closer again and revealed a dimple beneath that perfectly sculpted cheekbone. Rosanna stood immobile as he threaded the stem into her hair. He didn't touch her directly but she couldn't breathe. She remained still even after he'd finished. Because he didn't move. He just stood there looking into her eyes. And she looked back—unable to do anything else. The tension stretched. His expression was devastatingly hot. Was he really flirting with her? Did it happen like this—so quickly? So easily?

Guys never flirted with Rosanna. They never noticed her. And if by some chance they did, it was only to request to borrow her notes or to get something from the lab supply cupboard. And she definitely didn't attempt to flirt—too shy, too wary of awkward rejection. Relationships weren't something she had much experience with. Only right now there wasn't just a flutter of anticipation inside her, there was a fizzing sensation and a temptation to lean closer and say something...*stupid*, probably. Yet she couldn't seem to stop herself.

'You're not going to make me pay for it?' she asked. 'No punishment for petty theft?'

The terrible thing was she was curious as to what sort of 'penance' he might require—might it involve skin?

What was wrong with her?

His eyes widened slightly. That fizzing built the pressure inside her—threatening to explode in a way she wasn't sure would be wise.

'Why would I want to punish passion?' he asked softly.

Passion? An unfamiliar flare of heat swept over her. She felt passion for plants, yes, absolutely. But this was different. He was unbearably handsome, and his all-serious intensity called to something within her. Mortified at her thinking, she glanced away from him. Small talk wasn't her thing either. She'd always been shy, but she had to get herself out of this, quickly.

'It's an amazing view,' she muttered awkwardly.

He didn't reply.

'And it's the most beautiful terrace,' she added, her nerves growing. 'It's weird because you know you're in the heart of a massive city, but it's quiet and secret up here.'

She didn't usually fill silences. She wasn't usually around people long enough for awkward silences to develop.

'You've seen the other apartments?' he asked.

'The ones that are open, yes.' She glanced up at him and couldn't help a burr of defensiveness. 'I've not been sneaking through others. I'm not a thief.'

'No?' Something flickered in his expression. 'How do I know there aren't other things you've taken?'

That glint in his eye ignited a fire beneath her skin. A sense of playfulness—of challenge—filled her.

'You can't take my word for it?' she murmured. 'Or are you going to pat me down?'

She experienced a sudden craving for touch that was so strong and so unlike her that she shivered.

'I can imagine a strip-search.' His gaze grazed down her body as if he had X-ray eyes able to see through the black satin to the plain black underwear she wore beneath.

He was like a shadow in which you found danger— enter depths you might get lost in and thus never emerge into the sunlight again. Rosanna was most definitely lost already.

'The only thing I've taken is the frond,' she said.

'Why that one in particular?' he asked softly. 'I saw the way you looked at the plant—as if it was something precious. What makes it so special?'

How long had he been watching her?

Embarrassment curled. 'The coloration on the leaves. I wanted to see if I could grow it from a cutting,' she mumbled.

'So it wasn't just a whim?'

'I don't tend to do things on a whim.'

His eyes crinkled. 'Nor do I.'

She suddenly smiled because that she could well believe—he seemed too intense to indulge in spontaneity. 'I shouldn't have taken it without asking.'

His eyebrows lifted. 'We're all tempted to take things we shouldn't sometimes.'

His huskiness fuelled the fire of temptation already melting her.

'I won't tell if you won't,' he added softly.

That whisper with its promise of secrecy forged something between them. Something illicit. Something tempting. She had the feeling this guy could get away with almost anything. He had an aura, not just of power or command, but of unshakable capability.

'Do you do that often?' she asked.

'Not tell?'

'Give in to temptation and take what you shouldn't.' That heat scaled over every inch of her skin.

He hesitated for a moment before his smile emerged and went ever so slightly lopsided again. 'Not often, no.'

She believed him—the discipline, the decency, the duty, rolled off his demeanour.

'Although that doesn't mean I can't be persuaded

by the right person,' he suddenly added. 'A temptation strong enough.'

That frisson of danger reared again.

'You look strong enough to withstand any temptation,' she said. 'You look like you have a lot of discipline.'

He half laughed. 'Appearances can be deceptive.'

'But not everything in an appearance can be faked.' Breathing, real, right in front of her, there was no dispute that those muscles of his weren't honed. Muscles like that took work. 'Or are you saying you're not as strong as you look?'

'You think I look strong?'

'Yes. That's part of your job, right?'

He cocked his head, that smile flickering around his mouth. 'You look like a cat burglar. You act like one too. Yet you cry innocence.'

Rosanna blushed. She was more innocent than he'd probably imagined. A virgin at twenty-six—basically a mythical creature, right?

She breathed, wishing the heat would ease. Her skin was so pale that a barely heightened heartbeat showed up on her face as if she'd seen the most embarrassing thing imaginable. The merest hint of adrenalin in her system turned her into a tomato, which then clashed with the orange of her hair. Her awareness of it only made it worse. Her mother always recommended she smother her skin in make-up for contouring and complexion control. That way she could obliterate the millions of freckles at the same time and make her appearance smooth and inoffensive. She'd not bothered tonight. She should have.

She shrugged. 'There's nothing else I want to take from here.'

'No?' He almost pouted. 'Now that is disappointing.'

'What did you want me to take?'

'Anything really, then I'd have to apprehend you.' His eyes lit up. 'Or you could just take me.'

That tension twisted.

'I'm not strong enough to take you on.' Nor experienced enough.

'I think you're underplaying your attributes.'

What attributes were they?

But he was watching her, his head slightly cocked to the side, his indigo eyes glinting as they caught that tiny light.

She was swamped by a rush of something so primal, so fierce, it stole more than her breath. The crazy urge to kiss him was so overwhelming it scared her. 'I'd better get back—'

He took her hand, his touch instantly silencing her. That heat thickened. She didn't—*couldn't*—move, though his clasp was loose and she could've broken away easily. She stared up at him, lost in the unwavering blue of his eyes, stilled by the gentle rub of his thumb across the back of her hand.

He regarded her intently, his voice little more than a husky whisper. 'Stay a little longer.'

CHAPTER TWO

IT HAD BEEN a simple invitation, yet there was an underlying suggestion—an offer of something so much stronger that was unspoken. And Rosanna couldn't break from the stillness. It was as if she were locked in a resin sphere—in a perfect tableau of temptation.

'Just a little longer,' he added gently, as if coaxing a timid creature.

A thread of something new pulled tight deep within her. A thread of strength, of defiance. For once she *didn't* want to be timid or silent. She sucked in a breath. 'Why?'

His striking gaze drilled into her, seeming to seek knowledge while impressing his own will upon her. 'You know why.'

Did she? He still stroked the back of her hand with his thumb. It was the softest of touches yet it sent sparks up her veins and she felt a dragging sensation deep in her belly. An inexorable pull towards him. An inevitability that she couldn't deny. The desire—the need— for more of his touch. Only his.

Lust at first sight? Apparently it really was a thing and it was unbelievably strong. Yearning caused her to tremble—like an abandoned animal craving connection. Once again that thread buried deep within tightened. She didn't want to be meek. So yes, she did know why. Because she felt it too. And for the first time in her life she felt like acting on it. Because there was a perfection in the mystery of him—of her. A safety in which she could finally take a risk. To be swept off her feet.

'Please,' he muttered.

Not a whisper, but a low masculine request that both sought permission and promised pleasure.

Rosanna lifted her chin to look him more squarely in the eyes—reading the heat and intensity in his. Keeping hold of her hand, he reached out with his other to cup the side of her face. She so easily could've stepped back to avoid that more intimate touch. She didn't.

She released a harsh breath at the gentle rub of his fingers against her jaw, her lips parting as she exhaled. He stepped closer, an effortless glide into her space. Still she said nothing, nor did he, lost in each other's gaze, in the heat weaving around them, drawing them closer still.

So very slowly, so very carefully, he brushed his mouth against hers. It was the lightest, briefest of kisses. It should have been shocking. She should have stepped back. To kiss a complete stranger within only minutes of meeting him? It wasn't the sort of thing Rosanna did. But the second that mouth of his slid against hers? Rosanna was gone and all that remained in her place was a woman who craved more of the man standing before her. And at her soft gasp he returned. This time his lips lingered and her mouth parted. She heard the sound low in her throat. A growl of satisfaction that stoked something equally primordial within her. An echo of the most basic instinct of all. The drive for physical connection. Lips, tongues, hands. Suddenly they were entwined as the next kiss—kisses—engendered more heat and stoked more want. He released her hand only to immediately place his hand on her waist. His palm was big and sure and she couldn't resist leaning closer. She wanted to feel more of him. She wanted to let him take her weight. She trusted that he could. And he did. He pulled her close and kissed her deep—until she was wax in his hands, warm and willing and pliant. Then he lifted his head and she read the message in his eyes.

Want. Need. Now.

Yes.

It was as if time had entered a small loop creating this space all of their own. Their understanding was unspoken but she knew this was an escape for him too. She briefly wondered from what it was. He didn't seem as if he ought to have any great concerns, yet she was sure he did. A second later the thought evaporated. It didn't matter. There was only this. Only now. And it was perfect.

Every kiss fanned the flames building within her. The hunger mounted. She rose on tiptoe, pressing against his hard body, rejoicing when he cupped her bottom with both hands and pulled her closer still so his arousal pressed against her, turning her on even more. Awash with sensual excitement, she understood for the first time just what he wanted. She wanted it too. Sexuality. Pleasure. A physical fulfilment. For the first time, she truly ached for it. And her body moved purely on instinct to get it. In the arms of a stranger—it was madness. But she reached higher still on tiptoe, her body tumbling into his. He caught her, as she'd known he would. But then he spun them both and pushed her down. She sank back against the soft cushions of the lounger, exhilarated as he followed, keeping the contact of hands and kisses.

He touched her, saw her. Yet to her own surprise she wasn't self-conscious about her skin—because he seemed to like it, given the teasing way he was tracing the patterns of her freckles. And she knew her uneven waist wasn't noticeable in this dimming light, while her scoliosis surgery scar remained unseen as she lay on her back. She wouldn't have to mention it, let alone explain. Besides, he seemed to be focused on something else— something *within* her. Something far more important. Something raw. Something that sucked all his attention.

That need. That matched his own.

Desire surged through her as if a dam had been released. A froth of foam masked the dangerous swirl of desire deep within—this unstoppable drag towards him. Towards the heat bursting between them. This was new. This was undeniable and it was most definitely insane—a moment of pure risk. But she didn't care. Hidden in this shadowy, verdant corner, there was no stopping this magic beneath the stars. With skilful fingers he swiftly unbuttoned her blouse. Even though the air was warm she shivered and suddenly realised the threat of exposure.

'No one can see us?' she asked breathlessly. Privacy mattered. She wanted this to be theirs alone.

'No and there's no cameras up here,' he assured her. 'Motion detectors, yes. But not cameras.'

'You know your stuff.'

'It's my job to.'

He knew other stuff too. How to kiss her so she trembled. How to touch her so she moaned. He undid her bra, pushing the cups away so he could tease her tight-budded nipples. That hunger and need burned. But she squirmed as he slid those skilful fingers up her thighs.

'At least let me do this for you,' he muttered softly.

She understood he wanted to give her pleasure—and the novelty of someone wanting to do something for her? She couldn't resist—could only bathe in the attention, the wonder. She watched him as he hooked his fingers into the waistband of her panties and pulled, sliding them down and off, exposing her most private part to the air, to his eyes, to his touch. At the light skim of his fingertips across that so private part of her she melted. And when he levered up and slid down the lounger to press his lips to the place where his fingers had just touched…that was when she was lost completely. When he tongued her so intimately she was shocked into stillness and silence. But as his mouth sucked and his hands teased, he stirred the most agonisingly desperate feeling within her and she could only fall into his hold—trusting him implicitly to take care of her. And he did—with lush sweeping relentless caresses.

She knew it was madness for him too—his breathlessness, the slight shaking of his hands, the film of sweat on his skin, the passionate determination to please her. Just at the moment when she thought she could take it no more he slid a single finger inside and his tongue flicked across her most sensitive little bud. She closed her eyes and screamed as waves of ecstasy rolled over her.

Long moments later she was still flushed and shaking, awed by the intensity of what he'd done to her—what he'd made her do—to abandon all caution or reserve. But it had been so worth it. So deliciously, sinfully good—so good it should have been enough. Yet there was a pulsing sensation at the apex of her thighs, a slick hunger not quite assuaged despite the bliss still coursing along her veins. She opened her eyes and saw him looking down at her, his smile that little bit uneven, as if he wasn't used to smiling. But when he did—wide enough—there was that dimple. She couldn't help but smile back. For such a strong, serious-looking guy, he had a sweetness about him when he pulled it out. And if he could do this for her? She wanted the rest. With him. This once. Barely knowing what she was doing, she pulled him back up towards her. He braced his hands on the lounger either side of her, holding back enough to look directly into her eyes. His smile faded as the question flickered in his burning indigo-blue eyes.

'Please,' she muttered.

Not a whisper, but a low feminine plea that both sought permission and promised pleasure.

She felt his muscles flex in response. She lifted her head enough to kiss him, stroking her tongue into his mouth the way he'd done to her over and over. And to her pleasure and relief he met her, matched her, finally lowering to crush her body with his again. She groaned the second he did. *Yes*. This was what she wanted. All of him, encompassing all of her.

She relished in his strength. In the power of his

body over hers and in the power she was discovering within herself. That she could make this big, strong man tremble? Make him gasp? Make him moan? All with only kisses and caresses? She felt free to explore his magnificent form—she unbuttoned his shirt, loving the soft silkiness of his skin and the steely muscle beneath. She rubbed against him like that eager kitten who craved touch. She couldn't get enough of it now, couldn't get close enough to him. His hold on her tightened, his sweeping hands soothing her restlessness and the small sounds of desperation she'd barely recognised as her own.

'Easy, sweetheart,' he muttered. 'I got you. I'm not going anywhere until we're done.'

That promise—awesome as it was—still wasn't enough. She trembled with renewed passion. He huffed out a breath, suddenly pulling back to reach into the pocket of his trousers to retrieve a slim wallet. Fascinated she watched him extract a small foil square. Her breathing quickened. She hadn't even thought about contraception. Thank heavens he had. For a heartbeat she contemplated telling him but changed her mind the same second. She didn't want anything stopping this. Her sexual status didn't matter. It was nobody's business but her own, right? He probably wouldn't even notice. And she wasn't worried that he might inadvertently hurt her. He was gentle, generous, his touch like fire. She knew how much he'd wanted to please her just then. And maybe it was crazy, but she trusted him completely with her body.

And maybe, most of all, it was selfish, but she wanted this. She wanted him. Now.

He gazed at her, bracing above her again. Neither of them said anything. The kiss said it all. Here. Now. *Everything.*

She wanted to know what it was like to be had by him. She wanted to be held secure like this in the cage of his arms, beneath the glorious weight of his tight muscled body. A prison, a paradise, a weapon of pleasure that he suddenly, sharply wielded as, with a sure thrust, he took her final secret for his.

She gasped, shocked, and for a split second froze. So did he.

'This okay?' he gritted through clenched teeth, his powerful body rigid around hers. 'You're very snug, sweetheart.'

Releasing a tight breath, she gazed up into his eyes— drowning in that almost purple blue. She didn't want to tell him. Didn't want him to stop. She grasped him on pure instinct, pulling his head to hers. Needing his kiss as she needed oxygen. For life.

And he gave it to her—his lips coaxing hers. He slowed right down, giving her time to accept him, time to be overwhelmed again. She forgot the sharpness of his possession as somehow her own strength surged. That new thread within her scaled up into a cord of steel. And now she'd adjusted to the heady sensation of him pinning her to the lounger, she realised she had him caught too. Instinctively she'd curled her legs around his. He was locked within her body now, within her arms, and it felt so good to move against his magnificent form.

His lopsided smile returned and his eyes gleamed as she arched beneath him, learning to meet him stroke for stroke. He paused, rolling his hips against hers before he thrust deep again, setting off a maddening, delighting sensation that she wanted more of. She moaned as he did it again, her desire for retaliation igniting when she saw his smile of satisfaction widen and that dimple emerge. Her hands clasped him harder, her hips lifted quicker, both caught their breath. He arched, tossing his head with a growl as she flexed on him and felt her femininity surge.

They exhaled deeply in unison as pleasure bit hard. Sensations scurried through her with every rock and thrust of his body. She was melting, disintegrating, her form turning not to dust but glitter—she was a sparkling mass of euphoria. The urgency rose. A burst of energy rapid-fired from him and through her. Suddenly it was passionate and frenetic and utterly unstoppable. They ground against each other in ecstatic agony, seeking the release that was so, so close it was torture. He was so strong he overwhelmed her. His breath was rough and hot in her ear, his groans rapid and unfettered, his possession fierce and relentless until she was the one who came apart. She was the one who screamed, shuddering as the orgasm stormed through her like a tornado, shattering her completely. Only then did he unleash with a final fierce thrust, his guttural groan ringing in her ears.

CHAPTER THREE

ROSANNA'S SKIRT WAS rucked up, her silk blouse open at her sides, her bra undone, the straps hanging like ribbons at her elbows. Her hair was half fallen from its bun. And who knew where her panties were? Honestly, she didn't care. She was utterly undone—a breathless mess of wonderment—and she refused to allow any embarrassment to slither in, and no regrets either. How could she possibly regret something that had felt so good?

He was slumped over her, his heart pounding as arrhythmically as her own. She ran her hands beneath his shirt and across his back, feeling once more the powerful breadth of him. The sweat-slicked heat of his skin, the web of hard muscles beneath. Neither of them was fully naked, but the parts that were, where skin pressed against skin, were where pleasure pooled. He was still locked deep inside her, still feeling every aftershock of emotion shudder through her.

He lifted his head and looked at her and offered that lopsided smile. There was the tiniest hint of rue in his expression.

'That went a little further and a lot faster than I anticipated,' he admitted huskily. 'But it was amazing. Thank you.'

She nodded, unable to answer because she had a lump in her throat the size of Australia. She couldn't hold his gaze either. Not without her truth leaking out. Her emotions. Her gratitude. Her wonder. And already she felt the return of that low aching hunger. *She wanted to do it again.* She turned her head to hide that particular truth from him. And that was when she noticed the light flashing intermittently on the deck beside them.

He turned his head to follow her gaze, his eyes widening when the light flashed again. Abruptly he withdrew from her. Rosanna felt chilled the second he sat up. He stood and swiftly fixed his trousers before reaching down. His phone had fallen from his pocket to the floor. Face up, the screen flashed as notification after notification landed.

As he retrieved it and stood reading the messages, his face was illuminated by the blueish light. He was appallingly handsome—beyond movie star and straight into other planetary perfection. Because men this good-looking didn't exist in the real world…moreover men this generous with their attention weren't real. And sure enough, he was distracted now and, going by the frown deepening on his face, not in a good way.

She took advantage of his distraction to pull herself together—swiftly re-clasping her tangled bra, buttoning her blouse and smoothing down her crumpled skirt. She was still wearing her shoes so was spared the mortification of trying to find them, but she instantly abandoned any idea of finding her panties.

'I'd better get going,' she muttered awkwardly, walking towards the locked elevator before he had the chance to reply.

'Let me…' He huffed out a breath and rubbed his forehead.

She knew he was diverted now and she didn't want to be a bother to him. She didn't want to analyse this. Rosanna didn't talk much to anyone, certainly not about intimate things; she was too wary. 'I really need to get back,' she said quickly.

There was a moment when he looked into her eyes when she saw a hint of regret. But he didn't argue with her. He didn't stop her. Which made her quest to leave asap the right one.

Doing this was a one-off. She needed to execute her vanishing act now before the lights came on and reality was exposed. Because if she lingered the magical facade would crumble and reveal the slightly sad, drab reality. He'd find out she'd lied to him—by omission yes, but it was still a lie and she didn't like to lie. She was a guest, not a worker here. She was lacking in real social skills. He'd not seen her naked, not seen her surgery scar or her pale skin under bright lights. She wasn't beautiful in the way he was—she couldn't match his perfection. And as much as she might want it, there would be no replay— not one as gorgeously secret and somehow *safe* as that had been. So it was best to leave now before any of that morphed to the rejection she was sure was inevitable.

He swiped patterns on his phone and she heard the elevator whirr. Did he have access to the security system on his phone?

'I'm sorry. I have to get back to work,' he muttered. He was still serious and focused, just not on her any more.

'Of course.' She didn't want his apology or any regrets.

It seemed to take an interminable amount of time for the elevator to arrive. She stepped in the second the doors opened. She turned to face him, making herself lift her chin and look at him one last time. Because this was a moment she'd always treasure. But the moment had now passed.

Leo Castle gripped his phone so tightly it was a wonder the screen didn't shatter from the sheer force of pressure. Work was the one constant. It was what he did best. What he needed to do. Always. And he needed to get back to it now.

But he felt a terrible sense of frustration. That fragrant, stolen moment with this woman had given him the most intense pleasure he'd ever had and she tempted him to take more. They'd not even had a whole hour. But more time would mean more talk and from that the truth would slip out.

He'd misled her. He, who was used to other people keeping secrets, who had long ago vowed not to have any of his own. Yet tonight he'd been tired, and so, unusually for him, he'd kept his own truth back. Happy *not* to be Leo Castle for a few minutes. Not the boring, responsible, always working CEO. In a moment of weakness he'd wanted to be someone else. *Anyone* but himself so he could just enjoy a moment with a pretty little thief. Only that moment had become several more moments. Shockingly fast and intimate. Unstoppable. Undeniable. He'd had *everything*.

His half-brother, Ash, was the player, not him. Leo

Castle did not seduce strange women in secluded corners. He did not have sex on a whim without even knowing his partner's name.

Tonight he had. Damn it. Tonight he hadn't wanted to be Leo Castle. Hadn't wanted to be responsible and focused only on work. For those glorious moments he'd wanted to forget everything and it had been so easy with her standing before him with her kissable lips and big eyes, her firebrand hair and her breathless, blushing intensity. She'd fuelled the heat in his blood, the sudden onslaught of need that had overruled his reason from a single touch. And her trembling response had rendered restraint impossible. The only regret curling through him now was that he had to let her leave. And that he could never admit to her the truth. Not now. She would be angry with him—rightfully so—and Leo Castle didn't deserve forgiveness.

He never had. Never would.

Leo Castle could never escape who he was—a man who'd *failed*.

He suddenly moved, shoving out a hand to force the elevator doors to open again. 'Don't forget this,' he said huskily.

He leaned in enough to pass her the stem she'd snapped from the plant. He'd snatched it up from where it had been crushed beneath them on the lounger just before following her.

'Thank you.' Mortified, Rosanna took the cutting, unable to hide how badly her hand shook.

She must have lost it in her dishevelment and had

forgotten about it completely as the ramifications of her actions sank in. She'd just given her virginity to a complete stranger in a heated, thirty-minute exchange. Now a wall of heat enveloped her. *She didn't even know his name.* But she didn't want to. She didn't want to trade numbers with fumbling awkwardness. Didn't want to hope that he might get in touch with her…some time. She didn't want that inevitable disappointment. This magical moment was perfect just as it was, right? And it was over.

But he still didn't release the elevator doors. Her heart thudded painfully as he stared at her, the blue of his eyes all but obliterated by the stormy darkness of his pupils, the full curve of his lips almost sulky. He was so intense she forgot how to breathe again. But she made herself mutter.

'Bye.' She knew she was blushing and she willed him to release the doors and let her leave.

Instead he lifted his hand and brushed the backs of his fingers down her jaw. It was the lightest of touches yet that sizzle beneath her skin flared. Her resolve started to crumble and all she yearned to do was lean back into him.

That couldn't happen. She made herself step away, breaking the contact. He straightened and dropped both arms to his sides. As the elevator doors closed the last image she had of him was his gazing at her—fully focused, intense, devastating.

And desolate.

Her heart lurched but at that moment the elevator descended. She didn't stop at the party floor. She repeatedly pushed the button to take her all the way down to the ground, desperate to get out of the place entirely. But she didn't really run, she all but floated, her feet barely touching the ground as she fled with her perfect stolen treasure.

CHAPTER FOUR

Two months later

'I'M A FRIEND of his mother's. Of course he'll see me.'

'I really don't think this is a good idea.' Rosanna hurried alongside her mother, trying once more to change her mind. 'Ash isn't in charge of Castle Holdings, it's Leo Castle you need to speak to.'

'Him?' Her mother blanched. 'After all our years of loyalty, he won't even take our call.'

Rosanna's headache worsened and a horrible taste burned the back of her throat—a sense of impending doom making her physically ill.

She'd decided on the spur of the moment to come to Sydney to check on her parents. She'd been down a couple of times since their accident the weekend of the Kingston Towers party because neither had seemed themselves. Now she had unpalatable news she figured it was best to give it to them face to face. This morning she'd been informed that she'd not got the junior lecturer job she'd applied for last month. She'd really only applied because she knew she 'ought' to progress in her career at the university and at least then the stories her parents spun would almost be true. But she'd not got it—apparently she was 'valuable' where she was. Honestly, she was ignoring the part of her that actually felt relieved she'd not been successful and the fact that she didn't really want to teach those large classes. She'd planned to tell her parents first thing and get it over with, but she'd arrived to find her mother in a rage because Gold Style hadn't won the tender for Castle Holdings' new apartment building in Melbourne and, worse, their current contracts had been cancelled. So now her mother had a battle light in her eyes that put Rosanna on edge.

'Why do you need me with you?' she asked her.

But she knew why. Ordinarily, her parents were a formidable, forceful *pair*. Striking-looking, confident, consummate professionals at the art of mingling and making connections to sell their service. But they'd left her father in a slump at home—it was so unlike him not to want to fight for this. Rosanna hoped it was just him taking time to recover from the accident, but he had a pallor that worried her. He'd not been himself in weeks.

'You saw Ash recently,' her mother snapped as she stalked along the pavement.

'Oh.' Rosanna gulped.

During their interrogation after the Kingston Towers party, Rosanna had made the mistake of admitting to her parents that she'd caught up with Ash Castle. She'd been clutching at straws—desperately thinking of anything to avoid admitting that instead of 'schmoozing' possible clients and being seen by Leo Castle, she'd been upstairs having hot sex with a stranger, a security guard.

She still couldn't believe that had happened. Couldn't forget it either.

But truthfully her conversation with Ash had lasted all of twenty seconds before she'd pulled her 'just got to speak to someone' card to escape the awkwardness. Initially her embarrassment had resurged when he'd brought up what had happened between them all those years ago at school but, now she mentally revisited that brief conversation, it only confirmed her feeling at the time that Ash hadn't been his usual carelessly charming self. He'd been subdued and concerned enough to speak up, something he'd not done at the time. Perhaps he'd changed? She frowned, because she wasn't sure people *could* fundamentally change like that.

'You finally have an "in" with him again,' her mother said. 'He'll listen to you.'

No one had an 'in' with Ash Castle. The guy was reckless in both his business and personal life. He invested heavily in start-ups then pulled the pin the moment he maximised his profits. Plus, he slept with anything with a pulse before rapidly moving on to the next woman. Except for Rosanna, of course. He hadn't slept with her. He'd only asked her out because his dying mother had told him to 'be kind to her'. That truth still made her wince.

Ash Castle had been the glittering mirage of possibility. The 'ideal catch'. Back then Rosanna had wanted to emulate her parents' success—to show she could be the daughter they wanted her to be. That was through acquiring useful contacts, right? Ash Castle had been the ultimate useful contact. So even though she'd not been particularly keen on him personally, she'd cultivated a relationship in the way her parents encouraged and said yes to his invitation to the dance. Worst idea ever.

Because the video of him 'cheating' on her at the school senior dance had caused Rosanna's public humiliation. But it had been the berating, ongoing disapproval from her mortified parents that had wrecked what self-confidence she'd had left by then. It had been her 'fault' for not being a 'good enough' girlfriend to keep him. Nothing about her had reached their standards—she'd been too shy and awkward, too crooked—even post-surgery—and now she'd been a public 'failure' socially speaking. For her parents, where image was literally everything, it was the worst—especially in that 'crowd'.

And maybe she hadn't been a great girlfriend. She'd been flattered that he'd paid her attention and she'd tried, in Gold Style, to make it 'work' for her. But she hadn't *fallen* for him. Yes, her pride had been crushed, of course. But she'd realised that, not only could she never be as socially acquisitive as her parents, she could *never* be who or what *they* wanted. And that was what had really hurt. And while there was little she could do about that, she *had* decided that never again would she attempt any kind of arranged relationship, or put business considerations at the forefront of personal choices. Call her a fool, but she wanted someone to sweep her off her feet…rather as that security guard had.

It was weeks since she'd given that complete stranger her virginity and she still thought about it too often. Late at night when she ought to be asleep, parts of her body burned so badly she'd had to take cold showers. Which was probably how she'd got this niggly flu. And she'd actually caught herself daydreaming when she should have been concentrating in the lab—wishing a tall, muscular man would stalk into work and whisk her away with silence and a lopsided smile. As if that were ever going to happen. It was an embarrassing fantasy she could never admit to.

But that was irrelevant. What mattered was appeasing her mother and Rosanna was certain there was no point in talking to Ash about Castle Holdings business. It was Leo—the man in charge—who was determinedly shaking things up, who'd refused to award them the contract and cancelled all their other outstanding ones. From all she'd heard the half-brothers were fiercely independent and loyal only to each other. Which meant Ash would refuse to interfere.

'It's just one contract, Mum,' Rosanna tried to reassure her. 'You'll get another. You'll get way more.'

Her mother halted so suddenly that Rosanna had to backtrack three paces.

'I didn't want to tell you, but your reluctance leaves me no choice,' she snapped. 'In an attempt to leverage what we'd saved, your father invested everything into a different apartment complex. Not one of Castle's. The deal's fallen over already.'

'What?' Rosanna blinked. 'What do you mean *everything*?'

'Every last cent. While he was laid up with that broken ankle he had too much time to think. He borrowed against the business and our personal home.'

'He *what*?' Rosanna gaped. Her father had put everything they had on the line?

'We've been on the edge for a while. That latest redevelopment we did at home went over budget.'

Her parents were always redesigning their own home. They were renowned for never living more than a season or two with the same style, or even the same home. It was part of their 'brand'. Everything was staged to look perfect and up to the minute. As a child Rosanna had hated the constant change. She'd never been allowed to keep any of the things she actually liked—not even a favourite cushion. Then they'd sell the house and move on to another to start the process over again. They rarely stayed within budget, always picking the best, most eclectic, most luxurious of fittings and furnishings, making the ultimate show home for their design flair. They'd moved from one place to the next in the most coveted suburbs, chasing glittering prizes and awards—masters of reinvention. They refreshed, revitalised, made their homes and themselves perfect all over again. Home—like everything and everyone within—had to be the best of the best.

Rosanna was meant to be the best of the best too. They'd pushed for success at all costs—even down to using their only child. They'd only wanted one because more children would have interfered too much with their creative careers. They'd pushed her ahead of her years at school because they'd wanted her to be bright. They'd straightened, not just her teeth, but her whole spine in an attempt to perfect her scoliosis and been disappointed when it hadn't worked as well as they'd wanted. It was better, but not perfect. Not enough for them. She needed to be an accomplishment. *Their* accomplishment. And when she wasn't good enough as she was, they embellished the truth. They'd always had to do that with her...

The reality was she was awkward and didn't want to get involved with some suitable society guy in a mutually advantageous arrangement or basically a business deal. The one time she'd attempted it, it had blown up in her face. But it was what her parents had done. They had a business merger more than a love match. They'd pitted their acumen together and forged identity with activity. But Rosanna had decided, after the Ash Castle debacle, that if ever she were to marry, it would *only* be for love. Maybe it was naive or romantic, but she wanted to be wanted—for all that she was, and for all that she *wasn't*. Because she wasn't *ever* being a disappointment to her partner as well.

But now…had her parents' tendency to blow the budget finally caught up with them? Rosanna finally realised that not even the heavy make-up could conceal the stress in her mother's eyes. Their livelihood was in peril. It explained her father's dejection.

'So now you know why this is vital and I need you by my side,' her mother added. 'You're friends with Ash. All that money we spent on that school for you has to mean something. We're counting on you.'

Her mother's plan was preposterous. Apparently they would say they were 'just walking past' Ash's office… as if that were ever going to be believable. They had no chance of succeeding. Ash had wanted nothing to do with his father's business. But her mother was so fired up, her father a shadow of his usual self, and Rosanna still loved them and wanted them to be proud of her. She wasn't the son her father had wanted, not the beauty her mother had; she was never going to be some society princess or talented interior designer who could take over the family business. She *had* hoped her job would work out and even that had failed. So, this one last chance? She couldn't say no.

'Okay.' Rosanna nodded. 'Let's go.'

She tried to hold her head high as they walked into the tall building but she was wearing an appallingly pink vintage Chanel suit that was her mother's—as the jeans she'd travelled in weren't smart enough. So she who 'should never wear pink because of her red hair', she who also 'shouldn't wear anything too fitting' because it would highlight the irregular curves of her waist thanks to the wonkiness of her spine, was now wearing both. The imperfect things she was supposed to hide were glaringly on show today. But to Rosanna it didn't matter whether she hid her physical imperfections or not. *She* was imperfect. Yet she'd worked hard to be happy within herself—honestly? She'd been happy when she'd first seen the results of her surgery. It had been enough for *her*. But not them. Never them.

She sucked in a breath, trying to revitalise her low spirits. But she'd not got the job. She wasn't going to see the security guard again. Her parents were on the verge of losing everything. And now she had to face the source of her teenage humiliation for the second time in as many months.

Could her day get any worse?

Ash Castle's offices were in an ultra-modern building in the heart of Sydney. Taking a breath, Rosanna followed her mother and another couple of people into the elevator and pressed the button to take them to the top.

It was going to be mortifying but Rosanna had been through worse; she'd survive.

'Hold that, please!'

A peremptory tone made her spine tingle. She obeyed without even thinking, pushing the 'doors open' button down while the man strode in. Not a man—a muscle mountain. Rosanna stared, horrified. It was *him*. Indigo eyes, smouldering sensuality, her *secret*. Her blood began to sizzle but at the same time, she was melting with embarrassment. He was looking down at his phone, frowning again, the way he had that night just after they'd been together. She could only hope he'd keep staring at it for the duration of the elevator ride.

Of course, he didn't. He glanced up and around as the doors slid shut, his blue gaze landing on her after the briefest of seconds. His eyes widened, the pupils surging so quickly they all but swallowed those striking irises. But he said nothing. Rosanna turned to stare straight ahead but her wretched skin burned and she felt herself beginning to sweat. She held her breath but the elevator seemed to be moving stupidly slowly. One person stepped out on the third floor. The other on the fifth. That left just him and her mother. Was he heading to the top floor too?

From her peripheral vision she knew he now leaned against the wall at the side. She felt his gaze on her— burning through her like some horrible powerful ray-gun. Doubtless he was puzzling over why she was here. The real question was why was *he*? This wasn't Kingston Towers. This was Ash Castle's company headquarters.

Her headache was blasted away by a jolt of adrenalin and astonishment. She was acutely aware of her mother beside her. Nervously she shot her a glance only to be hit by another wave of astonishment. Why was her mother suddenly so pale?

The elevator chimed and the doors slid open but none of them moved. It was as if they were all frozen.

'After you, ladies,' he eventually said.

It should've been the epitome of polite, yet there was a drawling sarcasm about the way he said 'ladies'. It was unfathomable. Her mother hesitated then walked out onto the landing. But then she turned to face the man who'd followed them both out.

'You've not met my daughter, Rose.'

Rosanna's jaw dropped. Did her mother *know* him? But her mother didn't do the helpful thing and introduce *him* to her. He was the security specialist, wasn't he?

He glanced at Rosanna. His eyes narrowed and there was a stiffness in his stance that made her even more wary. He looked like a predator about to attack. There was no reason to attack. No reason to embarrass her—surely?

'Actually, Danielle, I *have* met your daughter. We met at the Kingston Towers opening. Didn't we, *Rose*?'

Time stopped completely. All Rosanna could hear was the rush of her own blood pulsing too fast.

'You did? Rose?' Her mother sounded startled and expectant for more information.

But Rosanna couldn't take her gaze off the man before her. How did he know her mother's name? Why did he look so grim? There was no sign of that dimple now, only cold anger. Suddenly she was afraid of what he might reveal.

'Briefly,' she said faintly.

Don't say it. Please don't say it.

That burning nauseous feeling returned. But he was still watching her and something raw flickered in his face before the rigid lethality in his gaze intensified.

'Is there anything I can help you with today?' he asked coolly. His glance flickered from her to her mother and back again.

Rosanna had lost all power of speech. *Why* would *he* be able to help them?

'No.' Her mother pushed the elevator button. It hadn't had time to go anywhere so the doors immediately re-opened. 'I've just realised we need to be elsewhere. I've got my meetings muddled. My apologies.'

Why was her mother apologising? Why was she so flustered and in such a hurry to leave?

'Actually, I wouldn't mind a few minutes to catch up with Rose again. Just *briefly*.' He stressed the word lightly but that lethal look in his eyes didn't lessen as he stepped nearer to her. 'That's if you can spare her, Danielle?'

'Oh?' Her mother sounded shocked and then shot Rosanna a sharp look. 'Then I'll see you at home later, Rose.'

Rosanna was too stunned to move but the moment the elevator doors shut—blocking her mother from view—the security guard grabbed her arm and marched her away from the weirdly absorbed attention of the two women staffing reception.

'What's going on?' she hissed as he opened a door.

He didn't answer. He guided her into a room and closed the door behind them both. Rosanna's uneasiness grew. Worse, so did the awareness within her body. Who on earth was he and what on earth did he *want*?

CHAPTER FIVE

ROSANNA GLANCED ABOUT the room, desperate to give her eyes respite and her brain a second to catch up. Ash's office was stunning, she had no idea how he got any work done with that view to distract him. Except it wasn't the view commanding her attention now.

'What's going on?' she asked again.

'Isn't that my question?' the tall security man countered as he leaned back against the door, blocking her exit. 'I have the impression you've not told your mother what really went down at the party.'

His choice of words was inappropriate. And deliberate. She fought off the immediate blush and inevitably failed.

'We came to see Mr Castle,' she said, ignoring the reference.

He stared at her fixedly for a moment. 'Mr Castle?'

'Yes. Ash Castle, the man whose office we're currently standing in.'

Why hadn't the receptionists stopped them? Where *was* Ash?

He blinked and lifted away from the door to take a step nearer her. 'Are you applying for a job?'

She bristled at his unfriendly tone. 'No, Mr Castle is a friend of mine.'

'You're friends with Ash?' His frown deepened. 'And your mother is Danielle Gold. So I presume your father is Red Gold, of Gold Style.'

She nodded. She had no idea why her mother had suddenly changed her mind about trying to see Ash. Or why she'd shot her that killer look when she'd left so quickly.

'And you're *Rose.*'

Why was he glaring at her like that?

'I prefer Rosanna,' she said stiffly, still feeling the heat of the flush in her face. Not that it was any of his business. She really didn't want to look into his eyes, but she couldn't break away from the intensity of his gaze.

He was staring at her as if she were a human Rubik's cube with one infuriating square that couldn't be turned into the right place. The silence stretched until she couldn't stand it any longer.

'Look, I'm here to see Ash—'

'He's not here,' he interrupted.

'Why are *you* here?' she demanded, patience lost. 'I thought you worked at Kingston Towers.'

He stared at her for another moment. 'You really don't know?'

'Know what?'

'That I'm also Mr Castle. I'm Leo Castle.'

She stared at him. *'What?'*

The reddening over his sharp cheekbones stunned her even more. People couldn't prevent blushing, she knew well. She blushed when she felt things strongly and when she had to admit awkward things. So what he'd said was true. He was Leo Castle—Ash's illegitimate half-brother. The man whose father had denied his existence for his whole life. Who'd fought for recognition and finally won it—the 'workaholic control freak' who'd taken over the company and terminated her parents' contracts. The man she was supposed to have *impressed* that night. The room tilted.

'No. That's impossible.' But the seriousness in his expression made her pause. 'You're not on the security team?'

'I'm on every team working in Castle Holdings,' he said. 'I'm the captain.'

'But you *told* me you were the security guy.' Her voice was a pathetic whisper, while a wave of anger arced and crashed through her.

'You *assumed* I was the security guy. I didn't correct you. Just as you didn't correct me when you told me you were working service that night. I soon found out that wasn't the case.'

Service.

She'd given him one sort of service, hadn't she? Oh, hell, it had been the most amazing moment of her life and the most intimate. And now he'd wrecked it—he'd *lied* to her.

'You know I wasn't?' she asked. 'You knew who I was?'

'None of the other waitresses knew anyone who matched your description.'

'You tried to find me?'

His mouth compressed.

It wasn't just nausea she felt now, but dizziness too. She swayed slightly and had to furiously blink.

Bad things came in threes, right? So here it was. She'd not got the job she'd been striving for. Her parents had lost their business. And now she'd come face to face with her one and only one-night stand—only to discover that, not only was he responsible for her parents' devastation, but he'd *lied* to her.

'Did you know who I was?' he asked.

She couldn't comprehend the question. Couldn't believe any of this was real. She'd been coming to see Ash Castle to support her mother. Even when she knew he wouldn't give a damn and would do nothing, at least she'd have tried. But this was Leo Castle himself. The man in charge. And if she asked him? After what had occurred between them? It was horribly sticky. Now she knew why her mother had left so quickly. She'd known they were facing defeat.

'Why did you want to see Ash?' he asked when she didn't answer.

She didn't want to go into it. There was no point.

'Tell me and I'll see if I can help,' he pressed. More than serious now, he was thunderous and definitely didn't sound inclined to *help*. 'Or shall I guess?'

She looked up at him.

'It's about the tender for the Melbourne building. And the cessation of Gold Style's other contracts with Castle Holdings,' he clipped. 'Are you aware of the reasons why they've been dropped?'

The floor seemed to be crumbling beneath her feet. She was suddenly on a precipice without knowledge or power to protect herself. Instinctively she knew he was going to tell her something she wasn't going to like.

The way her mother had abandoned her quest with such haste and discomfort?

'They betrayed Castle Holdings,' he said. 'Your father took confidential information to a competitor.'

Rosanna shook her head.

'They didn't tell you that bit, huh?' He watched her relentlessly. 'Moreover that competitor has already had several failed contracts and has been charged for breaking commercial law,' he said. 'I can't have Castle Holdings having anything to do with that mess. I won't have the name dragged into it.'

It surprised her that he cared so much about a name that his own father had refused to give him.

But she had to protect her *own* father. 'It sounds like he made a mistake. Maybe he was desperate and made a rash decision.' She shot him a pointed look. 'Haven't you ever acted on impulse?'

He met her gaze coolly. 'Not only did your father access confidential information that he gave to a direct competitor, he misrepresented his relationship with me to gain financial advantage for himself. There's no place for him or your mother in our structure any more.'

His coldness shocked her. He'd made up his mind and he wasn't going to change it. The awful thing was Rosanna could well believe her father might have talked up his connection to the Castle family. He'd talk *anything* up if he thought it would get him a sale. While he had a brilliant flair for design, he was not so brilliant in business—hence spending all that money on their own redesigns. And it was why the Castle contracts were so important. No wonder her mother hadn't wanted to face

Leo. She'd not told Rosanna the whole truth. Yet while she understood how bad it looked, how Leo must feel a sense of betrayal, Rosanna felt awful for her father too. He must've felt desperate.

'You hold my parents' livelihoods in your hands,' she said. 'Their reputation. Their life's work.'

Leo shook his head. 'Your father's own choices have led him to the position in which he now finds himself.'

'He's been unwell.'

'Then why not be honest?'

Rosanna could only answer honestly. 'Because he has a stupid amount of pride.' She sighed. 'They both do.'

'Can *you* be honest?' He watched her. 'Because you've just shown up to talk to my brother, who has *nothing* to do with my business. Who wants no input or influence. And you wanted to ask him to intercede.' His expression was stony. 'Did you know who I was that night?'

In the fairy tale, after her first experience of true lust, her life was supposed to have *improved*. There was supposed to have been some magical change—as if something had been unlocked within her—all positive radiance, right? That hadn't happened. In fact, her world had worsened. Admittedly, *not* because she'd slept with him. Rather because he'd just destroyed her parents' business. She knew it was wrong to hold him wholly responsible for that, yet at his questioning of her character now? She felt *furious*.

'I had no idea,' she said. 'None.'

He didn't believe her. The scepticism was clear on his face and the arrogant judgement of the man grated on her nerves.

'Was I supposed to have instantly recognised you?' she demanded.

'A lot of people do.'

'I'm not like a lot of people,' she said. 'I don't use social media. I don't read newspapers or watch much TV. Forgive me for not knowing your face.' She knew he still didn't believe her. 'Are you asking if I slept with you because of what you might be able to do for me in the future? If I used sex to get what I want?'

'Did you?'

She'd known he was going to ask but it shocked her anyway. 'That might be how you operate, but it's not my style. I had no idea who you were. If I had I never would've allowed what happened.'

'Never?' He suddenly smiled and it wasn't pleasant. 'What is it you think you know about me now that would change anything that happened that night?' He stepped closer. 'Because a name makes all the difference?'

'I think you know better than anyone the difference a name can make,' she replied.

He froze and his expression turned grim again. 'So you wanted to ask Ash to use *his* name and intervene?'

She couldn't answer that—he already knew.

'And why did she bring you along?' he continued sharply. 'Looking so very society princess in your pretty pink suit. Are you the temptation on a platter? The sweetener for the deal? Because you "know" Ash as well?'

That sick feeling swirled in her stomach.

Rosanna worried that in a way that was *exactly* what she'd been here to do. Not to support her mother, but to use a relationship to gain advantage. Only there wasn't quite the relationship anyone thought there was between her and Ash. Never had been. It was Leo who was the one she'd been intimate with. The only one.

Rosanna was feeling hotter and hotter and not in a good way. The perfectly air-conditioned office was stuffy. She wriggled her toes in her shoes but it didn't make any difference. The blood wasn't moving oxygen around her body. That dizziness swept over her again and trying to blink it away barely worked.

'Do you seduce many of your contractors?' she asked.

A spark ignited in his eyes.

'I think we could debate who seduced whom for hours and never declare the winner.' The muscle in his jaw twitched. 'The fact is we both won that night. You loved it. So did I.'

There was a roar of awareness at his assessment of their night. She remembered her pleasure as he'd come apart inside her. But that man was so far removed from the angry man standing in front of her now.

'Is it a weekly thing?' She persisted, refusing to succumb to those memories. 'Monthly?'

Grim. Furious. Still. He glared at her. 'Never before. Never since. You already know that.'

She fought the fierce pleasure his words brought, denying understanding anything of him.

'I don't know anything about you,' she said.

Except he was ruthless and unrepentant about it. And he had an unforgiving streak. He was not the wholly controlled, responsible man that people said he was.

'We'll put it behind us now,' she added determinedly. 'Forget it ever happened.'

'Do you believe that's possible?'

'Of course,' she lied. 'Now please let me leave.'

They didn't need to see each other again. *Ever.*

CHAPTER SIX

LEO DIDN'T WANT to believe her. Maybe he was arrogant, but people knew who he was. Given certain people had spent most of his life brazenly lying to his face, trust didn't come easily to him. Yet…no way was she that good an actress—the shock on her face when he'd walked into the elevator had been genuine.

His blood bubbled, heated by anger and by that other thing he was trying to ignore. But it was impossible to stop the memories spinning. He'd not been able to stop them all these weeks. They teased when he was too tired to resist. For a while he'd wondered if she'd walk into Kingston Towers again. He'd spent too many minutes indulging in that frivolous fantasy. He'd even briefed the security desk that if a blushing redhead ever appeared and asked for a security guy, they were to summon him immediately. She hadn't, of course. And now here she was attempting to go behind his back, to his half-brother, Ash. And what was their relationship, exactly? He didn't like the thought of Ash knowing this woman when he knew how the guy operated.

'How do you know Ash?' He couldn't help asking.

The wash of colour in her cheeks made him grit his teeth.

'We were at school together,' she said.

School acquaintances? Her blush suggested there was more to it than that. Jealousy flared instantly. He froze, furious with himself. Leo had worked hard not to be jealous of the half-brother who'd had everything Leo hadn't—legitimacy, two parents, the best education money could buy. But since getting to know Ash, Leo had learned those things weren't always all that awesome. He and his half-brother had more in common that they'd imagined, so he couldn't let this matter get in the way. His relationship with his brother was more important than this was.

'Ash isn't here,' he said harshly. 'He's in New Zealand with his girlfriend.'

Which was why Leo was in Ash's offices today. Ash had phoned for Leo's help with a work issue and of course Leo had agreed. He was happy the guy had worked it out with the woman he wanted. Even happier now, to be truthful.

Rosanna's eyes widened. Yeah, the words 'Ash' and 'girlfriend' hadn't ever been put together in a sentence before. But even that couldn't wash away the anger at the thought of her with Ash, no matter that it had been years ago. Ash wasn't having her again. *Leo* was. He'd make her forget any other man she'd known. He had to turn on his heel to mentally slap some sense into himself. Since when was he such a possessive brute? Normally he never gave a damn about a woman, never took the time to allow a relationship to develop. He was too consumed with work.

Only when he turned back to face her again there was that awareness in her eyes, an audible edge to her breathing. Electricity crackled—*emotion*. He didn't want *that*. Ever.

And he had no reason to feel guilty about cutting ties with her parents' company, right? That was a legitimate business decision. Her parents had shared sensitive commercial information, they couldn't be trusted, so he'd had no choice. And then they tried this—to go behind his back to canvas his brother and bring their daughter as, what, collateral?

It was unacceptable and unforgivable.

Rosanna hadn't known about her father's betrayal—that had been obvious as well. She'd been mortified. He understood the particular shame of having a parent who behaved badly. And a part of him also understood she wanted to protect and help her parents—that she was desperate enough to dress up in the hope of persuading someone. Leo could almost respect that, because he'd tried for years—doing all kinds of menial jobs to help his mother earn enough to keep them both. When it had got worse, when he'd screwed up, he'd been more desperate than to dress up, he'd literally begged for help. Only he'd failed. The difference here was Rosanna's failure wasn't going to kill her parents. No doubt they'd have another contract shortly, her father was too much of a salesman not to. It just wouldn't be with Castle Holdings.

What to do with Rosanna now? Those memories assailed him yet again, muddying his mind. He remembered the consideration she'd given to the garden, the secret sensual side of her he'd glimpsed.

'Did you grow a plant from that cutting?' he asked before thinking better of it.

Her eyes widened. 'Yes, as it happens. I did.'

It made him oddly angry. 'So, you got what you wanted from me and then you went after the other Castle brother for something else?'

Her pupils dilated even more and her face suddenly paled, making her freckles stand out shockingly against the paleness of her skin. His adrenalin surged as she swayed before him. He moved instinctively, drawing a chair close, concern overriding any anger.

'Sit down.' He cursed and firmly pushed her head down.

Rosanna felt atrocious. She battled to remain conscious and not sink into the velvety darkness. She was not *fainting* in front of this man. She choked back a rising bitter tide in the back of her throat. A glass of water materialised on the desk beside her.

'Drink,' he snapped.

She sipped it carefully.

'Most women swoon at my feet,' he said after a moment. 'They don't tend to turn green and gag.'

She chuckled weakly. 'I've insulted you.'

'Indeed, you have,' he said dryly.

She glanced up but there was no lopsided smile, certainly no dimple. And the mental image of all those women swooning at his feet worsened her head. But she had no right to be jealous.

He hunched down in front of her. 'Better?'

Indigo eyes. Intensity. So near. So gorgeous. And

she was so tempted to slide forward and hope that he'd catch her and pull her close.

She sat back instead. 'I'd keep your distance. You don't want this bug, it's nasty. I can't seem to shake it.'

'Oh?' He gazed into her eyes intently, that rich colour deepening. 'How long have you been unwell?'

She shrugged.

'Maybe you ought to see a doctor,' he suggested.

'Maybe I just need to go back to bed.' She winced the second after she'd spoken.

That intensity, bigger than them both, flared. She desperately tried to ignore that summons deep inside— it was like a clanging of a bell in medieval magical times, calling supplicants close. But something else flickered in his eyes and he suddenly reached forward and pinched the skin on the back of her hand.

'Ow! What are you doing?' She tried to pull her hand away but he gripped it tightly, staring at it. 'What is wrong with you?'

'What's wrong with *you* is the more important question,' he muttered. 'You're dehydrated. You've lost weight. You suddenly look like hell—' He abruptly stood. 'Come on.'

She stared up at him, half shocked and a little hurt. And, *no*. She wasn't going anywhere with him. 'What—?'

'Get up. We're going to see a doctor.'

'I am *not*—'

'Either you get moving and come with me to a private clinic, or I call an ambulance and we create an almighty scene in front of everyone. Your choice.'

He was too tall, too implacable and far too calm, all things considered.

Control freak. Her mother had been right. He was serious and determined and he wasn't going to waste time arguing with her.

'Who do you think you are?' she growled, but she stood anyway.

'A concerned citizen.'

The fact was, she felt terrible. Worse now that she'd seen him. 'This is ridiculous.'

She wanted to slink home alone all the way back to her tiny safe flat with her pretty plants and pet fish, far away from this overly bossy man who made dangerous feelings come alive in her traitorous body.

He wrapped his arm around her waist and guided her—as if she couldn't walk by herself. Dreadfully, she realised she did need his support; she was as wobbly as a barely set panna cotta. She was vaguely aware of the wide-eyed stares of those receptionists as they waited for the lift. Once inside he swiped a security pass and the elevator smoothly dropped them to the basement.

His sleek silver sedan wasn't like any car she'd been in. It was seriously low to the ground and the engine utterly silent.

'This is electric?'

'Yes.'

'You like it?' she asked. Distraction was good. She needed to stimulate the candy-floss-like capacity of her brain—it seemed to be dissolving as the seconds slipped by in his presence.

To her relief he actually took the hint and talked her through the specs, filling in the time with irrelevant facts. It felt like only moments later he swooped into a fifteen-minute car park. They were never going to be fifteen minutes or less at a walk-in medical clinic.

'You'll get a parking fine,' she muttered.

'I don't care.'

To her mortification Leo took over. It wasn't a drop-in clinic, it was *private* and they were happy to attend to her immediately. She was taken to a screening room with a nurse who documented her symptoms and took a few tests. It was ridiculous and unnecessary and she was mortified because now that Leo Castle—she was still getting used to *that* idea—wasn't in the room, she was breathing easier and feeling better. Now, she was embarrassed that he'd dragged her in here and caused such a scene, demanding that she be examined immediately. Not long after the nurse had left, the doctor appeared, closing the door behind him. The expression in his eyes made Rosanna's heart seize. The wariness about him scared her.

'Is something wrong?' She leaned forward.

'I have some results already.'

That was quick. The nurse had left the room only a few minutes ago.

'HCG was detected in your urine sample,' he added without further preamble. 'The blood test will indicate the exact levels and give us concrete confirmation, but it looks like you're pregnant. And that does explain your symptoms.'

Rosanna just stared at the man.

'Rosanna?' He spoke again. 'Did you hear what I said? You're pregnant.'

His voice faded as comprehension sank in. *Pregnant?* That wasn't possible.

'There's been a mistake,' she muttered.

The doctor sat in front of her and smiled. 'Have you missed a period recently?'

She didn't know—it was unlike her not to notice, but she'd been preoccupied with trying not to be distracted by memories of the man out in the waiting room!

'If you like we can do an ultrasound now,' the doctor added. 'That would confirm the pregnancy and give us a clearer idea of your gestation. Would that be helpful?'

She was coming across as an idiot. Shock did that to a person. And the thing was, if she *was* pregnant she knew exactly how far along she must be—she'd only had sex the once in her life!

'Would you like me to invite your partner in for the procedure?' the doctor asked.

Her *partner*? That dizzy feeling swarmed again.

Next second there was a cool damp towel on her forehead and the nurse was watching her. 'You're a little overwhelmed?'

Rosanna drew a deep breath. 'Can I have a moment alone with Leo, please?'

The door opened again only a second after she left. He must've been lingering near.

'What did the doctor say?' Leo asked calmly as he closed the door. 'Or do you want me to guess?'

She stared at him, picking up on something in his tone. He couldn't possibly have known *already*?

But he was staring at her fixedly. 'I'm right, aren't I?'

She was reeling from that test result while he looked like…an automaton. He couldn't know *everything*. No one did. He scared her. Not just how wealthy and powerful he was. But how *different* from the man she'd thought him to be that night on the terrace.

'What makes you so sure this baby is even yours?' she blustered, desperately needing some kind of defence from him.

He hunched down in front of her once more. 'Tell me it's not mine, then.'

She stilled because this time there was burning cold rage in the backs of his eyes.

'Will you lie to my face, Rosanna?' That relentless gaze was laser-like—stripping through her layers to seek the truth. 'Not just a white lie, not just an omission,' he added softly. 'Will you tell a life-changing, damaging lie?'

It wasn't just the shocking question or his masculine beauty. It was the seriousness and will emanating from him. He compelled her honesty by sheer force of personality. He wasn't someone to mess with and his honour called to her own sense of responsibility. He who she knew had been denied for so long in his life.

She couldn't lie. Not to him. Not to their child. Not to herself. Not ever.

'You can't *possibly* be so certain,' she said huskily.

'Why would you want to lie?' His expression was taut.

'Because you frighten me.'

He visibly paled. 'Why? You think I'm going to make you do something you don't want to?'

'I don't know.' She didn't know anything about him.

And yet she also realised that it wasn't him who frightened her. It was how she *felt* around him. Her response, her whole-body reactions were purely instinctive. Around him she behaved in a way that was so unlike herself. *That* was what was scary.

'We'll work this out, Rosanna,' he said. 'You invited me in here just now. You had a reason for that. A good one.'

'They want to do a scan.' She swallowed. 'They asked if you would like to be present.'

She stared at him, but he was so hard to read. How did he feel about it? His chiselled expression was stonier than ever. No lopsided smile. No dimple. But now no fury either.

'Of course,' he said briefly. 'If you're happy for me to remain, then I would like to.'

He was so polite, yet she was sure emotion simmered within him. But he was so controlled he wasn't going to let it out.

Somehow she survived the embarrassment of having the scan with him beside her. She stared at the enormous screen unable to see much in the swirling grey.

'Okay.' The doctor sent them a bracing smile, pointing at the screen. 'You see that?'

'Is that...?' Finally it appeared even highly competent Leo Castle was lost for words.

'There are two, yes.' The doctor drew a breath. 'Congratulations, you're having twins.'

'That's...amazing.' Leo turned from the screen to her. 'Isn't it, darling?'

Darling?

'You're about eight weeks pregnant,' the doctor added.

'Yes.' Leo cupped the side of her face and gazed right into her eyes. 'How wonderful.'

When he looked at her like that, the oxygen level in the room dropped and every brain cell slithered into hibernation, leaving her with nothing but the desire to lean into his touch. She was that clueless creature seeking heat from the sun.

'It's just incredible,' he breathed.

'Incredible' was correct. How could this have happened? And why was he looking at her as if—?

It's for show. This is for show. He doesn't mean it.

She belatedly realised he didn't want the medical staff thinking this was the shock that it truly was. He didn't want them to think this was a *mistake*.

Rosanna's blush burned because this was nothing but a pretence and for a second *she'd* made the mistake of believing in that look, in that intent. But this wasn't real interest. This was duty and responsibility and honour. Everything he'd fought for before.

Leo covered her hand with his and squeezed as if willing his strength to transmit through the contact. But it didn't stop the panic seeping into her. This was happening too fast. She hadn't even known his name a couple of hours ago, and now they were acting as if they were starry-eyed lovers celebrating the most longed-for pregnancy ever. The falsity of it was appalling. And the reality?

Terrifying.

CHAPTER SEVEN

ROSANNA COULDN'T THINK. Her not getting that job, finding out her parents' business was falling apart and learning her one-night lover was a total liar—wasn't that enough? But to find out she was pregnant—with *twins*—in front of him? That life as she'd known it had just disintegrated for ever?

She didn't listen as the doctor made suggestions for follow-up appointments. Leo agreed to something and then something else while she was too shocked even to pretend she was listening. Leo held her hand as he smiled and thanked the staff.

Somehow they were back outside. Somehow he hadn't got a parking fine even though they'd been more than an hour. Somehow she was in the car, her safety belt on, and he'd pulled out into the traffic, driving with a certainty she couldn't comprehend.

But in seconds she realised his fancy car was too small. She felt trapped in a myriad ways—on a journey, moving too fast with no idea of the destination or even when she might get a chance to take a breath. There was no way to slow this down.

'Where are we going?' she muttered.

'Somewhere we can talk.'

He'd dropped the facade of the deliriously happy partner the second they'd got into the car and she wasn't ready to talk about this yet.

'I want to go home.' She winced at her breathiness.

'Where's home?' he asked.

'Newcastle.'

'Fine.' He kept driving.

Rosanna stared at him. That was *hours* on the road. Hours in this too-confined space. 'I'm not driving all the way there with you.'

His jaw clenched. 'Can you just trust me to work this out?'

Rosanna wasn't sure she could or *should*. She should be assertive and take control of her own life but she was so shocked by the news they'd just received that she was almost catatonic. Whereas Leo was all 'action man'—decisive and fast, making it all too easy just to let him. Twenty minutes later they pulled up outside a charter helicopter business.

'It's a forty-five-minute flight.' He glanced at her. 'Give me a moment to arrange it.'

Less than a quarter of an hour later she was strapped in beside Leo while the pilot worked out the flight plan. She should have been excited, given this was her first helicopter ride, but she was too preoccupied to even feel nervous. Headphones muted the engine noise but she still couldn't think. She was so inwardly focused she saw nothing of the view. When they landed in Newcastle there was a car waiting. Leo ushered Rosanna in and took his place behind the driving wheel.

'What's your address?' he asked.

She gave it to him.

He plugged it into the navigation system, then frowned. 'That's the university?'

'I live in a campus flat there.'

'Alone?'

Her heart pounded. 'Yes.'

His hands tightened on the wheel as he pulled out into the traffic. 'What do you do?'

This was how little they knew each other. He didn't even know what she did for a job. 'I did my science degree here and never left. I work as a teaching lab technician at the school of Biological Sciences.'

'What does that entail?'

'As a lab tech I prep experiments for the students, do demonstrations for them. Make sure the equipment and supplies are maintained. I help the senior researchers run their experiments and record data. I also take tutor groups—mostly first year students, drilling into them lab rules and etiquette.'

'Biological sciences is what, plants?'

'More like petri dishes. I mostly work with the microbiologists.'

He asked a few more questions—more details of her duties. And then the kicker. 'Do you enjoy it?'

She hesitated but they pulled up outside her university flat before she had to answer. Rosanna was stunned by his efficiency, but felt no relief at arriving home—in fact she was struggling with having him in her small space. As she watched him assess her lounge with a single swift glance she knew she wasn't going to be able to stay here. It wasn't a place to raise one, let alone two babies. And she wasn't going to be able to hold down her lab tech job either. She was in real trouble.

'How long will it take you to pack enough for a week or so?' Leo asked bluntly. 'Because you can't stay here.'

'I can't leave,' she immediately argued. 'I have work, for one thing.'

'You can't work, you keep half fainting. Besides, you can't work around those chemicals any more, can you?'

She felt control slipping from her—she'd not even thought about that. There were protocols but she sensed Leo was a zero-risk kind of control freak. 'Then where do you expect me to go?'

'Seriously?' He stared at her. 'You know we need to sort this out.'

So the answer was obvious.

'You've not been taking care of yourself,' he added. 'You've had symptoms for days and haven't been to the doctor.'

Doctors cost money and she'd needed to work. She'd not wanted to put a foot wrong before that position was announced.

'Stay with me at least for a couple of days while we talk through how we're going to work this out.'

He made it sound so simple. But it wasn't.

'I'm not staying with you. That's not happening.'

'Then I'll stay here with you,' he said.

That was even worse. Her apartment was one bedroom and tiny and there was no way the man could stretch out on her sofa. Heat built in her cheeks. She refused to feel attracted to Leo. *Refused.* Except her damn body wouldn't listen to what her brain was screaming and responded to him regardless. Her eyes wouldn't stop looking. Her skin wouldn't stop tingling. Those secret parts heated…

'Or do you want to stay with your parents?' he asked coolly.

She froze. She'd forgotten all about her mother, who must be wondering what in the world was going on. The thought of telling them her news made her stomach roil. Not because they'd be disappointed, quite the opposite. She had the awful feeling they'd want to take advantage of her pregnancy with Leo Castle's children in a way that would be ludicrous, because everything to them was about bettering the business, enhancing their reputation and their aura of success and society. They would use this against Leo in their fight to win back those contracts. Suddenly she realised Leo knew that too. He must be *hating* this.

She pulled out her phone and saw she'd missed five messages from her mother. She'd put her phone on silent ahead of that terrible meeting that hadn't happened and, with everything that had gone so catastrophically awry since, she'd forgotten all about it. She quickly tapped out a reply.

I'm fine—will call later!

Then she switched it off. She didn't need to deal with a volley of messages back yet.

Leo watched her the entire time. 'You know we need to talk, Rosanna.'

She leaned back against her counter and moistened her lips with a quick touch of her tongue.

'You can't have nothing to say.'

For the first time she saw frustration gleam in his eyes, but his voice remained measured.

'What was that pantomime at the clinic?' She suddenly burst with anger. 'You were acting as if we were...'

'I don't want people talking.' He shrugged negligently. 'And I won't have what's mine kept from me.'

'What's *yours*?' Something stirred within her—an odd mix of rebellion and primal satisfaction of her mate signalling his protective intent. 'This is *my* body.'

'You're right, it is.' He advanced upon her. 'And I've seen first-hand how an unwanted pregnancy can ruin the life of a mother and damage the child irreparably. I won't allow that to happen to you. I promise you'll have whatever support you require.'

He was saying all the 'right' things yet somehow it made her feel worse. 'So you're saying I've won the unplanned pregnancy lottery?'

'I'm saying you'll never have to worry about whether you have a safe place to sleep, or enough money to feed your children, how to scrape together their sports fees, or pay for the constant clothes because they outgrow everything every three months.'

She suddenly realised that this was a *personal* list—that he'd really meant 'first-hand'. Because *he'd* been that child and those were real crises that his mother had faced. She knew some of his 'myth'—the battle to gain recognition as Hugh Castle's son—but she hadn't fully appreciated the real difficulties.

'I'm sorry,' she breathed.

'So am I.' He stood right in front of her like some fortress of strength. 'But accidents happen. It wasn't either of our fault, we just have to problem-solve the best way through it.'

He was moving too fast. His mind leaping ahead with a speed she couldn't keep up with—talking about clothing and food and shoes while she was still in shock.

'What do you want to do, Rosanna?'

Her heart thudded but her brain slowed again. It was as if his nearness lulled her into a false sense of security. That thread of desire tightened. As if everything would be okay if he kissed it better. It was shocking that, faced with the biggest crisis of her life, all she wanted was his touch. She desperately needed to get away from him so she could sort herself out.

'I need time to think. Space to think.'

He paused, then stepped back towards her sofa. 'Then I'll wait until you're ready to talk.'

'You don't trust that I'll come and talk to you when I'm ready?' she asked.

He briefly hesitated again. 'Don't take it personally. I don't trust anyone. Certainly not with my personal business.'

He was more of a stranger to her now than that night on the terrace. That night he'd been courteous, kind, generous...focused on pleasing her. Now he was revealed as a ruthless businessman with an uncompromisingly hard core. This was a man who'd fought relentlessly for years—forcing his father to accept his existence and claiming all that was rightfully his. He'd done it before so he'd do it again. Goosebumps rippled across her arms. It wasn't that he didn't want these babies. He wanted to be involved. *How* involved?

'Then I'm going into my room for a while,' she said.

'I'll support you,' he muttered as she moved. 'No matter what.'

It made her oddly angry that he was putting this decision all on her. He'd offered everything, yet in some ways nothing. This was life-changing and huge and completely terrifying. As she turned the handle and pushed the door, stepping across the threshold, he called to her.

'Fair warning though, Rosanna. I want these babies. They're mine. And I'll do all I can to convince you to have them.'

Leo watched her disappear into her bedroom, barely holding back the urge to chase her and haul her into his arms promising to do anything and everything to make her say yes to what he wanted. And what exactly was it he wanted? The primary instinct was to *protect*—both her and the babies. But the last thing he wanted was to ruin her life and he couldn't be sure he wouldn't. His existence *had* ruined his mother's life—at least for periods of it. And he'd *failed* to protect her and care for her when he was big enough, when she'd needed him most… He'd gone to his father and begged for his help only to be denied and rejected again and then suddenly, shockingly, it was too late.

So having a family—children—wasn't something he'd ever considered. He didn't think he had the attributes. His bloodline sure didn't seem to make good fathers; he'd figured he was better off not bothering. Besides, he was too busy with the businesses. He liked it like that. And babies? They were for a lifetime.

He released an uncomfortable breath. Everything

had changed. That control over his destiny that he'd been so smug about? *Obliterated.*

Too bad. This wasn't about him any more, but those babies. He was *not* letting them down. Not the way he had his mother.

All his childhood he'd been acutely aware of his mother's financial and emotional struggles even when she'd tried to hide them from him. He couldn't help Rosanna with emotional issues, but he could certainly help with financial. So at least in that way this outcome could be different. It could and would be so much better. It had to be. He wasn't having anyone else suffer because of his mistakes and, while this pregnancy *was* a mistake, he wasn't having his children believe their very existence was a problem or that they were ever a burden—not that his mother had ever said it. But he'd seen her struggle. And his extended family—her family? They'd made them both feel shame and guilt—and *unwanted.*

No, that wasn't happening to these babies. There would only be acceptance and enrichment—literally. At least he could deliver that.

Another wave of panic rose at the prospect of actually parenting. He had *zero* clue how to be a father. His mother had been amazing but his father certainly hadn't. He'd refused to admit he was even his father, let alone engage at all. And Leo hadn't been the amazing son his mother deserved. He'd let her down the moment she'd needed him most. What made him think he could do any better for Rosanna?

He didn't. But the very least he could give them was the security and safety that he and his mother had never had. *Financial* security and the safety of the Castle name would be like a forcefield around them. That had to mean marriage—the old-fashioned contractual kind where alliances were forged and kingdoms shored up. The political kind that ensured the safety of citizens. In this case, two tiny ones.

He just had to convince Rosanna. He glanced around her small lounge, gleaning what information he could, doing the diligence. Her flat was small but filled with life—literally. By the window was a tiered stand filled with pot plants while on a table in the corner was a tank with a lone, very odd-looking fish. He grimaced at the vitality. If it weren't for paid employees, anything alive left in his care would've long ago died of neglect. He was too busy with work to remember to water things and he travelled for long stretches all the time... Not great attributes for impending fatherhood.

He rolled his shoulders and looked the other way, but there was more greenery. On the dining table was another plant alongside a pile of notebooks. He couldn't resist peeking at the open one. Drawings covered the page—diagrams, to be precise—of the plant on the table. She'd written notes about it in very fine, neat writing. If she was a scientist, that meant she'd see reason, right?

Shut in her bedroom, Rosanna was a mass of contradictions. She grabbed a weekend bag and tossed it onto the bed, furiously dismissing the wicked thoughts that flashed in her mind when she saw her pulled-back sheets. How could she be thinking about getting hot and heavy with him again instead of getting to grips with how life-changing the revelations of the last hour had been?

She was *pregnant*. It was unplanned. She had no true partner. Sure, Leo would be there, but she sensed he meant that only in a business, 'problem-solving' sense. They didn't know each other. Intimately and emotionally she was on her own and, even though he said he'd do the right thing, she was sure that he didn't mean marriage. That 'right thing to do' wasn't required in this day and age.

But she *wanted* these babies. It hit her in a huge wave of emotion and instinct. They were a miracle. Awe burgeoned inside and maybe it was insane to be so rapt at this prospect, given her personal circumstances, but she wanted these children so much she had to suck in a steadying breath. She was just going to have to be clever about *how*. People all the world over were successful single parents. As long as she loved them and they were together, they would be okay.

But she couldn't manage on her own financially. Not now. She didn't have any savings. She'd been a student too long and her technician's salary was meagre. Her debt meant she'd have to continue to work and with childcare costs the way they were...? She couldn't ask her parents for support; they had their own crisis to face. Besides, she didn't want their unfulfilled expectations of her being transferred to her children...

The obvious answer was the one she most wanted to reject. Leo Castle had more money than he knew what to do with, but she didn't want to be *dependent* on him. He had the right to be involved and have his say, but she had to maintain her independence. And as long as she kept her own physical distance from him that would be possible. When he was near, when he was touching her, she couldn't think straight. She could barely think at all. There was no way she could keep her distance while they were here in her tiny flat. But she'd do whatever she had to, to ensure her babies' well-being.

He glanced up as she walked out of the bedroom.

'I think we should go back to Sydney to work through all our options,' she said briskly, as if it were her own idea. 'I'll stay in a nearby hotel.'

Not with her parents. Not with him. *Neutral* territory. She'd begin as she meant to go on.

'I have a spare bedroom. What's the difference?'

She gritted her teeth. 'Space.'

'My apartment is larger than most hotel suites. You'll have plenty of space.'

He wasn't going to give up, he'd argue every point. It was the 'sensible' thing to do and they did need to talk and no doubt his apartment was massive. Plus, it would save her money. She could control her base impulses, surely? 'Fine.'

'You'll pack your things?'

'I already have. I just need to sort the plants and Axel.'

'Axel?'

'The axolotl.'

'That weird fish?'

'He's not weird.' She put some food into his tank and made a mental note to text her neighbour asking her to check on him while she was away. It would only be a couple of days. Then she scattered some nutrients onto her plants.

'You don't have as many plants as I thought you would.' Leo came closer to watch what she was doing.

She sent him a sideways glance, not sure if he was being ironic. 'It takes effort so I'm judicious about my selections.'

'Really?'

For the first time Rosanna saw his dimple flash and something melted inside her. 'I like the unusual ones.'

'I can tell.'

'There's nothing wrong with something being a bit different,' she said softly. 'Or imperfect.'

'I'm not good with plants,' he muttered.

'They just need a little of the right attention.'

He studied her plant stand, his gaze following the plastic piping she'd fashioned. 'This is quite the set-up.'

'It means I don't have to worry about their heating and watering. It's all on a timing system.'

'You built it yourself?'

'I work in a science lab,' she said coolly.

'So you can make all kinds of clever things from all sorts of nothing?' He turned to look right into her eyes.

'It's just tinkering.' She glanced away from his intensity. 'And I don't have the funds or the space to just go buy a glasshouse. But I don't want them to die while I'm gone.' She grabbed her current notebook and a tin of pencils, putting them safely into the top of her bag, conscious that he was still watching her closely. It was causing her innards to overheat again.

They didn't speak on the helicopter flight back to Sydney but her heart pounded regardless. She knew Leo wasn't just *thinking*, he was plotting and preparing plans for their future. What he wanted, why he wanted it and why she ought to agree with everything he suggested instantly...

Possibilities circled through her mind and she tried to think of counter-arguments to what he might suggest, only she kept coming up short. With a sinking feeling she suspected she had little leverage. She could only try to hold her own.

CHAPTER EIGHT

THERE WAS SUCH inevitability about their destination, yet even so Rosanna couldn't stop herself asking as the elevator opened to let them out, 'So, this is your apartment?'

Kingston Towers penthouse. Inner-city paradise. Scene of her undoing.

'Yes.'

The worst flush she'd ever experienced swamped her. Her pulse skittered as intimate memories scurried through her mind. That was why he'd been here that night. Why he knew how to operate the slick security system. Why he knew whether there were cameras in here or not. The stunning secret garden with its hidden pool and soft lounger were all *his*. Compelled by memories and magnetism, she couldn't stop looking at him. She was drawn to him in a way she couldn't deny, not even now they shared a massive problem. He was watching her back. No smile, no dimple, but a fierceness in his eyes that made her catch her breath.

'I was going to sell it, but I couldn't help holding onto it,' he said quietly. 'I have a nice memory from the opening night party.'

Now that fiery colour wasn't just staining her cheeks but her entire body. 'Have you made more "nice memories" since then?'

It ought *not* to matter, but it did. Badly.

He slowly shook his head. 'I've had to make do with that one.'

She was swamped by a rush of hot relief and primitive satisfaction. He regarded her with that inscrutable stare and she had the scalding sensation that he too was remembering particular points of that evening and for a split second she thought he was about to—

Suddenly he turned and strode into the apartment. He carried her bag straight down a long corridor and into a large bedroom, devoid of any signs of occupation; she knew the room wasn't his. Still, she also knew his was too near. She should have insisted on staying in a hotel, because the tension simmering beneath her skin was too much.

'It's been a long afternoon.' Huskiness roughened his voice. 'You must be hungry.'

Yet to her the time had passed quickly.

'Rosanna?'

She'd just noticed the bedroom window overlooked the terrace garden and now her throat had clogged. Memories scalded—the scent, the taste… She *ached*.

'I'll go organise something,' he growled and stalked out of the room.

She attempted to think calming thoughts. Rational thoughts. In the luxurious en-suite bathroom she splashed her face with cold water. It didn't work. Her cheeks remained flushed, her mind frantic. There was no escaping the memories both he and the garden stirred.

Finally she walked out to the massive living area. It was dominated by double desks upon which there were several computer screens. All were switched on. His work was clearly his priority. When she finally made it to the kitchen he was putting a large tray on the counter. It was covered with gourmet sandwiches, tiny tarts, crackers, cheese and fruit.

To her surprise her mouth watered. 'How did you...?'

'The chef downstairs delivered it a couple of minutes ago,' he explained briefly. 'Shall we take it outside?'

She couldn't face that garden yet. 'Here is fine.'

With him on one side of the vast counter and her on the other.

Leo poured them both cool sodas and took a seat. Patient yet intense.

'Tell me what you're thinking,' he said when they'd both replenished a little.

She drew a steadying breath. At least now she wasn't blushing like mad. 'I'm not giving them up,' she said. 'I'm keeping them. They're mine.'

It was more than an echo of his own words. It was a challenge and they both knew it. He nodded but didn't smile. He didn't need to—satisfaction then determination flared in his gaze. 'That's a good start,' he said. 'Now we negotiate.'

She didn't think there was going to be much negotiation. There was going to be a decree from him and denial from her.

'You know there's one very obvious, very easy solution,' he began.

She watched him, waiting.

'You can't guess?' he prompted.

'I don't think I want to,' she muttered.

A small smile of appreciation flickered. 'We get married. Immediately.'

She shook her head. 'No.'

It didn't matter if bald, flat rejection was rude, it was a ridiculous suggestion. It surprised her that a man so future-focused and innovative and capable enough to be in charge of two successful companies would have such old-fashioned intention.

'Why not?'

'It's unnecessary,' she all but shouted. 'We can take care of them without being tied to each other in such a complicated way.'

'Isn't it more likely to get more complicated if we're *not* married?' he countered silkily. 'This is the most straightforward solution.'

Straightforward? He had to be kidding.

'Marriage will give these children legitimacy,' he began.

'That shouldn't matter.'

'It shouldn't. But it does. It did for me.'

She'd worried his personal circumstances might weigh on him, but there was a major point of difference that he was overlooking.

'But you're not like your father,' she said carefully. 'You won't turn your back on them whether we're married or not. Their experience will be totally different from what yours was. Our marriage is not essential.'

'I disagree.' Such finality. 'And you don't know—'

'Times have changed—'

'Have they?' he interjected coolly. 'Why would I want to take that risk? Why would I want my children to suffer from even a sliver of the judgement I was subjected to?' He pinned her with a gaze far fierier than his tone suggested. 'Why would you want that for them?'

'*Marriage* isn't about them. They don't need us to be married to have the security you want for them. They could still have your name—'

'It's not *enough*,' he shut her down.

That glimpse of emotion, of anger, made her pulse skip. She saw him draw in a steadying breath, trying to control his reaction. This wasn't easy for either of them.

He was serious and focused, but now the forceful side emerged. 'Do you not believe they deserve the best beginning in life?'

'Actually I'm determined they'll get *exactly* that,' she said. 'But the "best" is *not* shackling their parents together in a sham that will only end in tears and acrimony.' She didn't want an 'arrangement' that she would resent for evermore. Wasn't she allowed to want love?

'Tears?' His gaze narrowed on her.

She sensed him pivoting, prepping for another attack.

'I'm not saying we have to sleep together.' He softened his tone. 'We can live separate lives.'

What did that mean—to be married and yet, not married? Didn't he want to 'have' to sleep with her? Even for that, she wasn't enough. Her anger flared. 'Are you saying you'll cheat on me?'

His mouth thinned. 'Of course not.'

He was too perfect, wasn't he? Too determined not to make the mistakes of his father.

'Then are you saying you can live without sex for

as long as we both shall live?' She batted her lashes at him. 'Because if we have to marry at all, then it must be for life, right? Otherwise why are we bothering?'

A muscle jerked in his jaw. 'If you're saying you expect this marriage to last, then that's wonderful. That's exactly what I want. We are in perfect agreement.'

'We are not!' She glared at him. 'You'd settle for a celibate life?'

A smirk slowly spread on his face. 'As I'll be married to you, I won't need to.' Dimples in both cheeks appeared while a glint lit his eyes. 'Our past record makes me think that I won't have to wait all that long for you to ask me to consummate our marriage.'

What? She stared at him, her jaw dropped at his arrogance. And the mortification that he *knew*…so she *had* to deny it. 'You'll be waiting an awfully long time.'

'Will I?' His smile vanished and he shrugged carelessly. 'That's fine too. I don't fool around all that much. I never have.'

'So no partying? No endless stream of beautiful women?' She'd suspected he wasn't a playboy but he really wasn't bothered by the prospect of a sexless future?

'I haven't the time to be frivolous,' he dismissed the question.

'You just work. A lot.' Which concerned her just as much.

'I like work. I'm not going to apologise for that.'

So very disciplined. So very controlled. Her fingertips itched. She didn't want him to be so damned *perfect* about everything. 'All work and no play…'

'Work *is* play for me.'

'Really?'

'Don't you love what you do in the lab?'

She didn't want to answer that honestly. He sat back, his smile building almost back to dimple point. 'Perhaps you'll use this as an opportunity to figure out something you love doing more?' He mused as if it were all an amazing chance she should be grateful to have. 'You won't need to work, so you can consider anything.'

Was he bribing her now?

'We're not in love,' she muttered.

'What has that to do with anything?' he blithely shot back. 'It may as well be you. Especially given the current circumstances.'

'It "may as well"?' She gaped at him. 'Don't you want to fall in love and get married for real one day?'

'Marriage has never been on my to-do list,' he said. 'But I can adapt when necessary.'

His denial surprised her. Had he never wanted to settle down with a life partner? Yet he was the ultimate catch himself—intelligent, successful, brain-fryingly attractive, not to mention stupendously wealthy. Women must target him all the time.

'You've never wanted a wife and children?' she clarified.

His expression shut down. 'It's not something I'd have gone out of my way to achieve.'

To *achieve*? As if it really was an item on his to-do list. As if, should he decide to, he'd just make it happen—all so easily. Which was exactly what he was trying to do now. He was a person of action and achievement—in every area. She wanted to rebel against that. Because she so totally wasn't.

'But that's what you want?' He cocked his head,

something flickering in his bright eyes. 'To fall in love? Are you a romantic, Rosanna?'

It didn't matter. Right now she had to be a *realist*. Because unfortunately the only guy to have swept her away on a tide of desire was standing right in front of her, offering her something utterly unpalatable. She wasn't going to have much opportunity to meet anyone else, given she was going to be busy on double-baby duty. Which was fine. Because she was going to have her children.

Leo looked tense. 'You want a happy marriage like your parents had?'

She nearly choked. Her parents were married to their *work*—and only by extension to each other. Nothing mattered more to either of them than their business, so they were a *partnership* that was far more professional than personal.

He, too, seemed married to his work. So, no, she didn't want that.

'I don't want to be trapped in some political marriage where we don't actually want to be with each other but we're together for societal reasons. That wouldn't be good for the children. They're not stupid.'

'It would only be unpleasant if we were actually warring, which I don't think we'll do.'

So he thought this would be some bloodless, cool-headed, passionless union? That might be true for him, but for herself? The feelings he aroused within her were definitely passionate. Definitely not cool-headed. And while he thought they could still sleep together— maybe—he didn't seem that *desperate* for it. Perhaps that night wasn't as memorable for him as it was her...

He watched her thoughtfully. 'Perhaps there are some other issues that could be solved if you agreed.'

'Oh?' She narrowed her gaze on him. 'Such as?'

'Our children will have security and safety.'

'They can have that without us being married.'

'They're my heirs. I'm a wealthy person. They might be targeted.'

She rolled her eyes. 'We're in Australia, not a lawless state full of bribery, corruption and kidnapping cartels.'

'It's still a risk I'm not prepared to take.'

'Then we live in one of your buildings.'

'I don't wish to be separated from them.'

'You want to be a hands-on father?'

He stiffened. 'I wish to be involved in their lives. For them to know who I am. And that I will do all that I can for them.'

What did that mean, exactly—*all that he could*?

He seemed to turn to stone before her eyes. More remote. More serious. More determined. 'It could be very advantageous for your parents should we marry.'

Her skin iced but deep beneath her blood began to bubble. The irony was that this was exactly the kind of socially advantageous marriage her parents had hoped she'd make. The reason why they'd sent her to that insanely expensive school was to meet the children of insanely wealthy people and foster connections that could enhance their careers. They wouldn't be outraged on her behalf at this proposal, they'd be pushing for her to say yes. The second they found out about the pregnancy they'd probably march over and demand Leo 'do the right thing' and marry her. They would use their newfound, blood-bound relationship to the Castles for professional gain. Use their grandchildren as they'd used her. They'd interfered in her social life once before and it had been mortifying. She would effectively be a bought bride. But under his sufferance too—he'd endure it because he 'had' to 'do the right thing'…and that would be hideous.

'In what way?' she asked coldly.

'They wouldn't need to worry about their work any more,' he said.

'Are you saying you'll renew their contract if I marry you?' she asked, unsure how she was keeping her voice steady. 'Am I hearing you correctly? A bartered bride, that's what you're going for?'

She didn't want to be anyone's burden—not less than one hundred per cent desired. So, no, she was never going to marry him. Never going to have a marriage of convenience.

He paused. 'There's no need to be so emotive. We're floating ideas. It's part of problem-solving.'

'By taking one thing utterly unrelated to this issue and using it as leverage?'

'I'm saying they wouldn't need to worry about losing their house.' He frowned. 'They need never work again. Early retirement, isn't that everyone's dream?'

So he'd not renew the contract. He'd simply pay her parents to go away. The outrageously wealthy man's answer to all problems.

'Is early retirement *your* dream?' she asked.

That frown deepened. Yeah, she didn't think so. Her parents lived for their work, just as Leo seemed to. Paying them to head off into the sunset wasn't any way to coax her into agreeing. And that he'd hold her parents' future fortunes over her made her think less of him.

'None of your reasons are enough to induce me to say yes to a crazy proposal,' she said bitterly. 'I would've thought a successful businessman like you would've been able to think a little more creatively.'

Right now Leo wasn't thinking at all. He was staving off the very basic, very wrong urge to *kiss* her into submission. He'd not known he suffered from caveman tendencies, but they were rising to the fore now and it was horrendous. He shoved them back down, gritting his teeth,. What frustrated him most was that this wasn't even an argument—she'd given a flat rejection from the start and stubbornly refused to entertain any good reason why she should reconsider. He'd come up against brick walls before. In the end he'd battered them down—destroying them in the process before rebuilding something better suited to his needs. He'd have to do the same here—because he'd do *whatever* was required to secure what he wanted.

Except what he wanted right now was off the rails. His body was trying to overrule his reason and push him into action. With the shock of everything today he just wanted a moment to feel good again. Getting close to Rosanna would feel more than good. Instead he stood rigidly, rejecting the urge. Look where succumbing to that lust had got them already.

Besides, he had to back-pedal over his mention of her parents. The fury that had ignited in her eyes? Mentioning them had obviously been a mistake, but he'd felt compelled to use whatever tools he had to secure his win. Except all he was doing was making her angrier and less agreeable. Unfortunately the spark in her eyes was making it hard for his brain to work. The flush in her face was fuel to his own flame, messing with his already reduced ability to rationalise his way out. He just wanted to touch her skin, trace the patterns of her freckles and flushes.

He was an animal, he really was. To be thinking about sex right now?

He had to focus on the imperative *need* of his new responsibility. He would give her and their children the security he'd not had. He would never turn his back on them. But tangible support was all he could offer. Financial security, physical safety and name. Nothing more. Certainly not happy ever after.

Because he was not a romantic. And she? She'd not answered that.

It was too bad for both of them, because marriage was the one and only structure in which all those things could be achieved.

The years he'd spent fighting to prove his own damn provenance? His desperation in trying to help his mother? She'd worked so hard to support him with no help from her family and none from his father. She'd been cast off when pregnant and his father hadn't just refused to admit or accept responsibility, he'd made her situation so much worse by denigrating her character. And Leo *had* been a burden for her—but she'd carried him, cared for him and he'd loved her for it. As soon as he was old enough it had been the two of them side by side together. But he'd been stupidly arrogant and eventually let her down with foolish, youthful laziness.

When she'd died he'd vowed he would get justice for her. To him that had meant proving her truth against the lies of Hugh Castle. It was the least he could do when he'd failed her so completely—failing to get her the help she'd needed soon enough.

And he couldn't help himself from working his ass off to make something of himself in the futile hope of getting just the attention, let alone the approval, of a father who was never going to be interested no matter what he did...

Not being given a chance at all? *That* angered him more than anything. And it felt just the same now, as if Rosanna wasn't giving him any kind of chance with her instant refusal of everything.

'You don't think it's an abuse of power to make such an offer?' She slayed him with the cool fury in her pale blue eyes. 'Maybe you're more like your father than you like to think.'

Cold anger washed through him, equalling the rage he read in her expression. How *dared* she? He r*efused* to be like his father. *That* was his whole point. His offer was the exact opposite of what Hugh had done. She wasn't thinking straight. Nor, to be honest, was he. It had been a long, shocking day. Rosanna needed a break. He, too, needed time to recalibrate and figure out the way to convince her. Firing off now would only worsen things. He refused to lose control of his emotions. Instead he made himself count to ten.

It barely worked. But he steadied enough to inwardly acknowledge that mentioning her parents was a kind of coercion. Even so, he didn't quite care. He'd use whatever it took to secure the future of his children.

He had to draw another breath. He could barely envisage them, or barely cope with the idea of not one but two small babies. Hell, he wouldn't know the first thing to do with them. *Caring* for them? That was impossible. He'd failed at caring for his mother. With devastating consequences. So he *needed* Rosanna to be onboard. He needed *her* there. This, the woman who nurtured broken plant cuttings to new life, all health and vitality. She'd know what to do with the babies. She'd fill the emotional gaps that he couldn't, and he would get her financial help. He'd hire her an army of nannies if she needed it. In this way they could be a good team. She just needed to understand that somehow.

Rosanna stared as Leo's eyes darkened with emotion. Had she scored a hit? Yet she felt bad; she didn't truly think he was anything like the two-faced cheat Hugh Castle had turned out to be. But his offer put her on edge, making her wary of what else he might try.

'It's not an abuse of anything,' Leo finally answered unevenly. 'It's a very generous offer. One you ought to consider seriously before it's taken off the table. You mightn't like what the replacement offer might be.'

Her skin chilled. 'Replacement?'

He shrugged. 'If I start going more "creative" with my thinking.'

A frisson of danger sparked in the stormy atmosphere.

But then he almost smiled. 'I don't want to argue with you.'

'No?' She couldn't take her gaze off him. 'You just want everything your own way.' She stood up from the stool. 'I'm not marrying you. Ever.'

'Why not give us a chance?' He too stood and walked around the counter.

'There is no us,' she muttered. 'There's just a…situation.'

'But there could be.' He advanced closer and the glint in his eyes froze her. '*You're* the one not thinking creatively now.'

She couldn't think at all any more. Not when he was this near, this intense, this determined.

'Why can't we make it what *we* want?' he asked softly.

Want?

Rosanna couldn't breathe. There was lightning now—fully charged attraction that was impossible to deny yet too much to bear. All because he'd come to stand right before her. Of all the people in the world, why did her body want him? A man who was bossy and authoritative and serious? Why this unemotional, ruthless, unforgiving man? Yet she'd just sparked to life.

'Don't look at me like that,' he growled.

'Like what?' she snapped back at him.

'I'm angry too,' he muttered. 'I'm frustrated as *hell*.'

Some long-secret part of her had taken control of her limbs. She didn't step back when he stepped closer. She didn't flinch. Didn't resist. Because the balm of having her body against his? She practically melded against him. It was like that night—when one touch had been all it had taken. His arms clamped more tightly at her wordless response. She couldn't stop staring. His mouth was in a grim pose yet perfect in its fullness. There was the slightest hint of stubble on his sculpted jaw. The angles and planes of him were honed and hard, yet there was a silken quality to his skin. That sizzling ache within soared.

He released a low groan and smashed his mouth over hers. It was the most appalling relief. She was flung into that furnace of molten want. The horrors of the afternoon were blasted away.

This was how to feel better. *This* was the only way to forget everything. She trembled against him, satisfied only when he pressed her hips against the heat of his. Finally feeling that rigid arousal again, she moaned. It was *madness*.

'Say yes,' he breathed.

It was such a hot whisper. But she realised it was seduction. Calculated. The *one* way he could get her to capitulate. Not just to say yes, but to *beg* him to do as he wished. Which meant it wasn't as uncontrolled as it was for her. And it would only be a matter of time before he lost interest. And that would hurt her.

'No,' she muttered back.

It was barely audible even to herself but he heard. He lifted his head and gazed down at her.

'Why not?' There was a gleaming darkness in his eyes now. A possessive wilfulness. He wanted her to surrender to this.

'It would be a mistake.'

'It's what we both want. I can taste your hunger, Rosanna. And I know you can feel mine.'

His bluntness was shockingly arousing and she was unable to deny the liquefying heat he aroused within her. She was so close to surrendering to what she wanted.

'*No.*'

He immediately loosened his hold before pausing

briefly to support her while she recovered her balance. She was mortified that he felt her trembling—that her body gave her away even when her words did not. But he respected her words. He didn't challenge the rejection as a lie. But there was an edge in his expression that made her wonder if she weren't in more trouble now than if she'd given way moments before. Because there was no denying the truth any more. There was only stopping herself from acting on it.

CHAPTER NINE

ROSANNA DREAMT SHE was trying to stop a waterfall with nothing more than a sieve…and there was an inevitability about her own drowning. *Twins.*

Her eyes flashed open. It felt impossible to do alone and she had no other support she could count on, which meant negotiating some kind of arrangement with Leo. A lifestyle that *she* could live with. That was not marriage, nor was it an affair.

She'd gone to her room immediately after that kiss last night. He hadn't stopped her—as if he too had needed respite from the tension. But she was sure his frustration was mostly concern for the future, whereas hers was complicated by the lust overtaking her every time she so much as looked at him. She *couldn't* marry him. Instinctively she knew the magnetism drawing her to him would hurt her eventually. She needed space to settle them into a platonic arrangement. Something peaceful, calm, *unemotional*. That would be best for everyone.

She dressed in loose jeans and T-shirt then opened the door that led directly from her bedroom out onto the terrace to appreciate the gorgeous morning sky.

With the door open she could now hear splashing and couldn't resist investigating. Leo was swimming in that small pool. It should've been impossible given the size, but there was some kind of machine humming. He must have seen her because he suddenly flipped to swim onto his back.

'I can set the resistance,' he explained. 'I can make it harder or easier, depending on what I need.'

Clever.

'So you're swimming to nowhere?' She tried not to stare at the bronze skin and flexing muscles on show and opted to tease him instead. 'Expending all that energy only to stay in the one place?'

It sounded hellish frustrating but no wonder he had that broad-shouldered physique.

'It's a good challenge,' he said.

'Yet so unrewarding. Never getting anywhere.'

'It's not about the destination though, is it?' He waded to the edge. 'It's about the process. The benefits of the journey.'

It just sounded exhausting to her. She'd constantly striven to prove herself to her parents, to her teachers, to her bosses…and ultimately her process, her attempted journey to acceptance, had failed. But Leo Castle wasn't a failure. He was the ultimate achiever.

He pulled out of the water and she couldn't stop staring. She'd not seen him fully naked that night. It had been dark and they'd both remained partially clothed. Now, in the brilliance of the early morning sunshine, he was all smooth skin and rippling muscles that gleamed with the promise of heat and silken pleasure.

'Do you feel better for a good night's sleep?' he asked.

What sleep?

Glancing up, she read heated amusement in his eyes. And heard the tone of arrogance.

'I feel marvellous,' she lied. 'What about you?'

'Oh, yes. Fully refreshed and ready for round two of the marriage debate.'

Did he have a knock-out move planned? Rosanna had to dig in for the long haul.

'But breakfast first, hmm?'

That chef from downstairs must've stopped in again because the outdoor table was laden with delicious options—creamy yoghurt, cereal, fresh fruit and still-warm pastries. Rosanna sank onto a seat, unable to resist.

But Leo's phone chimed three seconds after he joined her there. 'Excuse me, I need to answer this.'

She listened as he walked inside. His voice was low and reasoned—problem-solving, answering questions. Apparently the marriage argument wasn't his priority. That was good. Rosanna could appreciate the warmth of the sun and that stunning view across the harbour and the frankly amazing apple pastries.

Ten minutes later he returned. Her resting pulse rate picked up again even though he'd put on a T-shirt. She had to get a grip. But he'd barely sat back down before his phone rang again. As he walked around the terrace she could hear him instructing some poor soul to write up a report and have it to him within the hour. It was early Saturday morning and he was working—almost every minute of it so far.

Fifteen minutes later she carried her used dish to the kitchen, passing through that lounge where the computers were running, their screens filled with data and graphs and scrolling tickers along the bottom. He was now seated at one of the large desks. He controlled not one, but two large companies, which meant he had a lot on his mind. Work was his passion and that was fair enough. But the impact on children? She knew too well how it felt to be low down on the priority list.

Deep in thought, she went back to her room and freshened up. When she re-emerged over an hour later, he still hadn't moved.

'Still working?' she asked as he typed something out onto one of the three computers.

He glanced up for a second. 'Why does that sound like a loaded question?'

'My parents are workaholics. So I know it's not fun for kids.'

'There's nothing wrong with wanting to do a good job.'

'No. But balance is important.'

He sat back, a small hint of amusement in his eyes. 'Will this be your next reason to refuse me? I'm too committed to my business?'

As a child she'd been basically abandoned for business so her concern wasn't as petty as he made it sound. She knew how it felt not to have someone who took the time to *listen*. Who was always preoccupied and too busy at 'more important' appointments to bother turning up to her school events.

'I don't care about your business. If that's your priority in life, that's fine,' she said. '*My* priority is now

my children. And I'm not going to let them suffer by
having an absent, workaholic father, where everything
they do is dictated and determined by how best it is for
the business, around your schedule.'

He inhaled sharply. 'But the business is what pays
for the food, the roof over their heads.'

'Oh, please,' she sighed. 'You could retire this instant and have enough money to live on for a hundred
lifetimes.'

He blinked. 'A lot of people depend on me for *their*
work.'

'Because only you can be the boss?' She shook her
head. 'Maybe you should hire more people and free up
your own time.'

'I'm good at what I do, Rosanna,' he said softly.

Oh, she knew that.

'But isn't it awfully arrogant to assume that no one
else could possibly do your job as well as you can?' she
asked innocently.

'Not arrogant,' he denied. 'Nobody *cares* about it to
the same extent that I do.'

'Again,' she challenged, 'isn't it arrogant to assume
no one else could feel things as strongly as you do?'

'They've not invested the blood, sweat and tears that
I have. Or the years.' He leaned back in his seat and
surveyed her. 'It's about ensuring the right decisions
get made.'

'And only *you* can make them? You need to approve
everything. I bet you're an absolute micromanager. I feel
sorry for your staff.'

'Oh, there's no need,' he said with cool smugness.
'They're very happy.'

'Are they?'

'Given what I pay them, I'm certain of it.'

All the money for all the hours? For being able to drop everything first thing on a Saturday morning and write up some report for a demanding boss?

'What style of management do you think they'd prefer?' He rose out of the chair and strolled towards her.

She was on shaky ground here. 'Perhaps they might prefer a more collaborative approach. Or be allowed more freedom to work on problem areas themselves before coming to you. Perhaps they'd like more trust put in them.'

'And you're a successful manager? Employee? You have a proven track record in such things?'

She stiffened, not wanting to let him know that she'd failed in securing her promotion, yet she felt as if he'd guessed already. 'I just think that any kind of obsession is unhealthy.' She dodged his question.

'Ah.' He nodded and stopped just inside a safe distance from her. 'Perhaps. But obsession is how things get achieved.'

Because it was all about achievement?

'There's nothing wrong with single-mindedly pursuing your passion,' he said intensely. 'Not letting anything or anyone stand in the way of what you want most.'

What did he want most? Was it money and status? Conspicuous success?

Except right now, it felt as if he wanted *her*. And he was embarked on a single-minded pursuit like a hunter who wouldn't rest until he'd captured his prey. But it was only because he wanted her to say yes to the rest of

Complete the survey below and return it today to receive up to 4 FREE BOOKS and FREE GIFTS guaranteed!

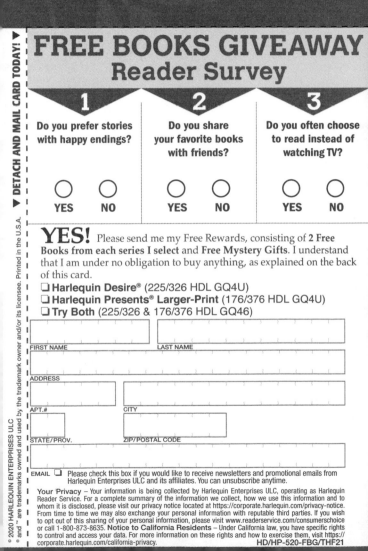

▼ DETACH AND MAIL CARD TODAY! ▼

FREE BOOKS GIVEAWAY
Reader Survey

1
Do you prefer stories with happy endings?

○ YES ○ NO

2
Do you share your favorite books with friends?

○ YES ○ NO

3
Do you often choose to read instead of watching TV?

○ YES ○ NO

YES! Please send me my Free Rewards, consisting of **2 Free Books from each series I select** and **Free Mystery Gifts**. I understand that I am under no obligation to buy anything, as explained on the back of this card.

❏ **Harlequin Desire®** (225/326 HDL GQ4U)
❏ **Harlequin Presents® Larger-Print** (176/376 HDL GQ4U)
❏ **Try Both** (225/326 & 176/376 HDL GQ46)

FIRST NAME — LAST NAME

ADDRESS

APT.# — CITY

STATE/PROV. — ZIP/POSTAL CODE

EMAIL ❏ Please check this box if you would like to receive newsletters and promotional emails from Harlequin Enterprises ULC and its affiliates. You can unsubscribe anytime.

the deal. The fine print of for ever. Inking an agreement that wouldn't do either of them—or their children—any good in the long run. And therefore one that she couldn't agree to.

'What happens when you finally attain it?' she asked. 'For how long does it keep you happy? How long until you start to think…this isn't that great. This isn't enough…what then?'

'There's always another challenge. That's life.'

Right. There would be another woman one day, who would be a challenge for him. And Rosanna wasn't sure she could stand by and watch that.

'So you launch from one challenge to the next. Relentless in your pursuit of achievement. Do you know how to relax? Do you ever take holidays?' She studied him. 'When was the last holiday you took? Never?'

'You make it sound awful when really it's not. I *like* work. I'm lucky.'

'Because you're alone and your single-mindedness isn't impacting on anyone close to you.'

He stiffened as she continued.

'*I* want balance,' she said. 'I want my children to have parents whose *lives* are balanced. Who can be there for them.'

His jaw hardened. 'And I *want* to be there, Rosanna. That's what I'm asking for.'

'A piece of paper isn't being there. Can you be there in the right way?' she persisted. 'Look at you, you're glued to your phone. You work every hour there is. It's Saturday morning and you're present but not really *here*.'

He was still for a moment and then he suddenly

smiled. 'You want me to pay more attention to you.' He put his phone on the table and stepped closer. 'That's fine, Rosanna. I can do that.'

She ground her teeth together. Not *that* kind of attention. This man wasn't like anyone she'd ever met. He was structured, disciplined, ruthless and relentless and so damn serious. And while part of her respected him for it, he scared her. She needed to know there was more to him than concern for spreadsheets. 'That's *not* what I meant.'

Leo watched her stalk back to her bedroom. Huffy and beautiful with her fiery hair tousled and emotion staining her cheeks. Of *course* it was what she'd meant. She wanted him. He wanted her. That part of it at least ought to be straightforward. He'd been frantically trying to focus on anything other than her all morning and he'd failed and he was frankly stunned that he was still struggling to secure her acquiescence to anything. The frustration of trying to talk to her while having his own mind hijacked by the demands of his body was killing him.

He'd been buying time to get his head around the situation by avoiding her this morning—giving her space too. Apparently that had been a mistake. But there was no damn rulebook for how to play this situation. The way his imagination slipped was highly unusual for him. Taking those work calls had actually been respite—a breather to recalibrate. His self-control had never been in doubt before and he hated it. And now she was calling him out on his method of *management*?

That frustration rose higher. This was everything

he'd never wanted—trying to understand someone, to make a relationship work? He'd never wanted to feel responsible for either the fortunes or happiness of anyone else again. Not after he'd failed his mother and lost everything.

But, damn it, he still wanted to pick Rosanna up, as if he were that caveman, and toss her onto the nearest bed and keep her there until she'd agree to his demands. There weren't many—to let him in, to let him have her...

It was some primitive instinct rearing, right? A ridiculous one at that.

This was not the time. Even though she'd responded to him last night he knew she was scared. He'd seen the strain in her eyes just before and couldn't forget her pallor when they'd been in that clinic yesterday. It had been primal instinct pushing him to touch her—to reassure her that it was wonderful. He'd said it was to stop people talking, but really he'd just not been able to help himself. A twin pregnancy was harder, higher risk, wasn't it? He swiftly searched the Internet for the information he had no idea about. Apparently in early pregnancy she needed rest, good nutrition and little stress. Arguing with him wasn't going to help anything. So he needed to back off and figure out a better way.

While their physical attraction was about the one thing they seemed to have in common, and he didn't think either of them were going to be able to resist it for long, last night she'd said no. Even when he'd felt her fiery response to his kiss. Even though she'd been as breathless and as into it as he. He'd swear on his life he wasn't wrong about that. But that night at the Towers she'd quickly left and never returned. She'd had no interest in learning his name. She'd only wanted to share a brief moment with him… *Why*? She'd obviously not been playing the ingenue. She'd have said yes to his proposal already if she'd had any sort of cunning plan. Which meant she was as unsophisticated as she appeared in those baggy jeans and tee this morning.

He remembered her blushing shyness, her nervous attempt at small talk, then the suck of her breath as he'd entered her snug body. A high-speed one-night stand didn't make sense for her. Maybe she was wary because more than the pregnancy was new to her…? Maybe she'd been more than overwhelmed just by their passion. Maybe she'd had less experience in the intimacy of lovers?

A sharp sensation of protectiveness—of possessiveness—speared through him. That *couldn't* be right.

But his instincts honed in. He *needed* to discover the secrets lurking just beneath her beautiful, blushing surface. Was he right? Because it might explain some things…

Suddenly escaping everything seemed like a fantastic idea. Perhaps he ought to take her criticism as constructive feedback. Perhaps he ought to take a break from work to focus solely on this situation. He could barely work anyway because he was too busy ruminating on her rejection. He couldn't concentrate until he got what he wanted. And now what he wanted was to know her. They could go somewhere warm with water and a beautiful view of things she liked—plants? Weird fish? And no interruptions whatsoever. He'd put all his energy into securing *this* deal. It was like any other acquisition, right? It needed time for negotiations; he needed to make the most enticing offer he could and the other party needed time to adjust to the change.

But there was no professional protocol to be maintained when the deal was this personal. He would protect his children. He would protect their mother. Somehow he would find a way to ensure she couldn't refuse what was right and best.

He phoned Petra—his assistant manager on the insurance arm.

'Sorry, P, I know it's Saturday but this is a biggie.' He gritted his teeth, thinking of what Rosanna had said.

Petra's surprise was audible as he asked her to step in and take over for a few days. But he also sensed her determination whistling down the phone. She wanted to do a good job. He knew he could count on his people, he just…hadn't done it to this extent before.

'I'm going to be out of contact almost completely,' he warned her, bracing against his own discomfort at the thought.

'For how long?' Petra sounded staggered.

'It shouldn't be more than a week, but I'll keep you posted.'

Then he phoned Jake on the Castle Holdings arm and repeated the request. It was only going to be a few days. Surely nothing too drastic could happen in that time. He'd sort out the marriage situation with Rosanna and prove her wrong about his micromanagement tendencies at the same time. Win-win.

He found her perched on the edge of her bed, frowning at a book.

'Did you unpack your bag already?' he asked.

Her eyes widened. 'Um…'

'Pack it again. We're going away.'

Her eyebrows shot up, like a porcupine on instant defence. 'Yesterday's travel wasn't enough for you?'

'I think you were right,' he said briskly. 'We both need time and space to sort this out *together*.'

'What about your work?'

'I can't remember when I last had a holiday.' Fact was, he'd never had one. 'Now is as good a time as any.'

A mutinous gleam shone in her eyes. 'So what's your plan?'

Was that resentment at his authoritative style? He breathed out, trying to slow down long enough for her to get on board. 'Where would you like to go?'

He'd already made arrangements but they could be changed—he could nail *adaptation* for her.

'I'm not leaving the country.'

Her suspicion was sobering. He had a lot of work to do to gain her trust. 'I'm not asking you to,' he said quietly. 'But we could get some fresh air and sunshine.'

'Have you noticed my skin?' She gestured to her face and body with her hand. 'The last thing I need is sunshine.'

Now he smiled, because he *had* noticed her skin. He couldn't seem to resist fantasising about tracing her freckles. 'Warmth and rest, then. You're exhausted.' He held his breath.

She regarded him steadily for a long moment. And then? 'Okay.'

A win. *Finally.*

CHAPTER TEN

ANY OTHER WOMAN would consider a three-hour flight cosied up in a first-class pod with Leo Castle a dream come true. For Rosanna? It was a nightmare. He was too close; she could smell the freshness of his soap and feel the warmth of his body. Both of which made her want to lean even closer. She didn't, of course. She fretted.

She'd messaged her parents just before boarding, guiltily telling them she'd gone away on an assignment for work. It wasn't altogether untrue. This was a kind of business. And she wanted any future arrangement agreed with Leo before telling her parents. She didn't want them attempting to interfere.

'Why the Great Barrier Reef?' she asked Leo, desperate for distraction from his nearness.

'Why not?' he replied. 'You ever been?'

She shook her head.

'Me either.' He smiled enough for the one dimple to make a brief appearance. 'We can discover it together.'

He was working hard at being agreeable but the truth was there was a slender bond of intimacy growing between them. Not quite the sort she secretly ached for. Right now she couldn't maintain eye contact or she was going to do something stupid. She pounced on the small packet of snacks the air steward passed her. It was exactly what she needed to occupy herself. But the packet was impossible to open. She tried with hands, then teeth, then with pure unadulterated frustration.

'Do you want—?' Leo broke off as the foil finally burst and launched salty rice snacks into the air like confetti. 'A hand with that?' He finished the offer belatedly.

Rosanna stared. *Leo* was the one who needed a hand. He'd borne the brunt of the explosion. A billion rice snacks now littered his lap. She half expected *him* to explode next. Instead he shot her a sideways look and not one, but two dimples appeared. Next minute, the man was laughing.

Rosanna remained frozen a split second longer, then she too slid into a chuckle—half in relief, then pure ridiculousness. His laugh was warm and infectious and the unexpected merriment multiplied. She giggled helplessly as she felt his shoulders shake in an easy, intimate moment. She helped him collect the morsels, trying not to make anything of the chance to touch him, but she felt her flush building and knew he was watching her expression too closely.

'Sorry,' she muttered.

'I'm not,' he answered in that low, intimate way. 'It's nice to see you laugh. You haven't much.'

She glanced up and was ensnared in his gaze. 'Nor have you.'

Now he was smiling, small and lopsided, but true and unbearably intense. The whisper of want swirled, spinning her closer to him. It would be so easy to tip forward and touch her mouth to his—that kiss last night had sent her soaring. And his smile now reminded her of the gentle humour that night on his terrace at the towers. It had been irresistibly *easy* then. But they'd both been pretending to be people they weren't. That wasn't reality now.

'Next time, let me help?' His gravity washed through her like shock waves, radiating through her body to bone.

Could she trust him to? Did she have any real choice?

In *how* he helped? Yes, she did. She sobered completely and made herself sit back. She had to think more clearly than this.

After the flight they faced a hop by helicopter. They skimmed over sapphire waters, looking down on emerald and gold islands that Rosanna could scarcely believe were real, so gorgeous were the colours. Finally at their secluded destination, she stood on the deck just absorbing the hombre blues stretching before her. The privacy and luxury and untouched wildness were profound.

'Lost for words?' he asked quietly.

She nodded. She'd thought that by escaping the city—his domain, her family difficulties—she'd be able to focus on combatting his will. Only now she was here in this incredible, unique beauty, peace descended. In a place this perfect, there could be only tranquillity.

'We have the hut to ourselves,' he said.

Rosanna smiled. She wouldn't exactly call it a hut. The stunning villa was mostly open-plan with clean lines and soft furnishings that subtly screamed comfort. She'd noted with relief that there were two bedrooms, both with stunning views. They had their own pool as well as that amazing ocean just behind her. But none of these exquisite things were enough to distract her from the man now walking towards her.

'Give me your phone.' He held his in one hand and stretched his other towards her.

'Why?'

She followed him into the villa and watched him open the small safe secreted in the lounge. 'Locking away my phone and my watch. Yours too.' He glanced at her wrist but she didn't have a fancy smart watch like his.

She met the challenge in his gaze and handed her phone over.

'No phones. No moans,' he mocked.

'What?' She coloured at his amused phrase.

'That's the deal, right?' he said softly, standing too close to her. 'No work. No pleasure either. At least, not sexual.'

Her heart beat heavily.

'Because, just so we're clear, that's how *I'd* like to relax,' he said.

He actually looked more relaxed already. More handsome. More tempting.

'You said you didn't really fool about all that much,' she muttered huskily.

'Now I'm here with you I can't think of anything better.'

She tried to breathe. '*Not* going to happen.'

'I know.' He grinned. 'I'm resigned to the fact.'

But *she* wasn't; instead she was already battling the heated thoughts his words conjured. 'You'll never last without your phone.'

'Maybe *you'll* never last,' he countered. 'You'll be the first one to give in.'

'Is that your goal? To make me the one to surrender?'

'Surrender?' His lips curved seductively. 'Why does it have to be a fight when it's something we both actually want?'

'We all want things that aren't good for us sometimes.'

'Sometimes we just need to live a little because who knows what's going to happen tomorrow?'

As they had that night at Kingston Towers?

'How long are we staying?' She desperately turned the topic.

'A week or so? Thought we could play it by ear.'

Her pulse lifted. She was going to be alone with him for *days*. 'Wow. That's a long time for you to be away from work. How are you going to cope?'

'I'm sure I can find some way of passing the time.' Such loaded implication in a quiet drawl. His smile suddenly flashed. 'You enjoyed it, Rosanna. Why not let yourself enjoy it again?' He leaned closer to whisper. 'It can hardly make the situation worse, can it? You're already pregnant. We're already in a mire of complicated. Why do we have to feel frustrated as well?'

So this was merely a source of frustration for him? 'You don't think it will make things worse?'

'I think it will make some things a whole lot better,' he said calmly. 'At least it will be out of the way.'

She stared at him. 'So you think it will go away?'

'When you've had enough of anything, you don't want it any more.'

So *she* would become something he could take or

leave without any concentration or effort or will. He'd indulge but couldn't foresee indulging in *her* for too long. It wasn't as if anyone else had ever wanted to. But for Rosanna the amount of will required to resist *him* right now was almost unsustainable. And if they indulged, what if they then became out of sync in the satiation of this hunger? What if he'd had enough before she did and he didn't want her any more? He would find someone else who he *did* want. And…what if she never had enough? What then?

His smile softened. 'I'm going to go cool off,' he said. 'You want to join me?'

She drew a steadying breath. She shook her head. 'I'm going to…eat something.'

She watched him disappear into one of the bedrooms and then went to the sleek kitchen counter. She'd not considered how intimate this trip was going to be. How it *had* to be. She couldn't play a part, she had to be herself. It was inevitable he'd discover everything about her here—it was the point, after all. Which meant she had to show herself as she was—flawed, stilted. Usually she was okay with herself, but she felt a flutter of nerves at him seeing her in a swimsuit. Her loose jeans and cotton tee were enough to mask scars—but she had more than scars to show.

She put together a small plate of delectable snacks from the vast selection on offer in the fridge, then went outside and sat on the comfortable lounger on the deck by the pool. She determinedly lifted her gaze beyond the pool to the amazing water beyond. Remote and isolated, this was an escape from the rest of the world and coming here was truly bucket-list material for her. She couldn't wait to explore the living reef; the aquatic life would be incredible. Except at this moment she was most fascinated by the man tirelessly swimming length after length as if a great white shark were after him. He was in there a long time and, incredibly, her lashes lowered as the sound of the water and the warmth of the setting sun and the oddly comforting closeness of Leo Castle lulled her and suddenly she was fast asleep.

Rosanna stretched out slowly, loath to relinquish the dreamiest sleep she'd enjoyed in weeks. But as she blinked she heard an amused voice from a distance.

'I was wondering if you were ever going to wake up.' Leo stepped into her line of sight. 'You're like Sleeping Beauty.'

She stared at him—his black swim trunks and red tee revealed strength and heat... 'Holiday' Leo looked *fine*.

Quickly she sat up. 'But I'm awake now. No kiss necessary.'

She was still dressed in yesterday's jeans and tee but she had no recollection of getting from the lounger outside to the bedroom. He must've carried her and she didn't even remember it, which was...*embarrassing*.

'You were very sleepy,' he said.

She glanced down beside her, noting the smooth clear space where he'd not slept.

'I took the other room obviously,' he added, revealing yet again he'd read her mind.

She felt that wretched heat fill her face.

'Although you're far more biddable when you're half-conscious.' Amusement kindled in his eyes. 'Like a little limpet. It took some manoeuvring to extricate myself from your sleepy clutches.'

Surely he was joking? But she could well believe her body would burrow close to his given the chance.

'Don't worry, I was a gentleman.' His customary serious expression returned. 'I'm sorry if all the travel was too much.'

'It wasn't,' she said huskily. 'I was just tired.'

He left her and Rosanna resolutely put on a bikini she'd barely worn and covered it with a wrap dress. She couldn't pretend to be anything she wasn't and the sooner she was honest with him, the better. On her way through she snaffled a pastry from the platter on the kitchen counter and went out to the deck. It was a stunning day. Leo had sunglasses on and was pulling together swimming gear from a room by the pool.

'You want to explore the reef after breakfast?' he asked.

'I'd love to.' She studied one of the masks. 'But I'll need to practise in the pool first, I've never snorkelled.'

'No?' He glanced up at her in surprise. 'You grew up in Sydney, right? City of swimming pools and beaches.'

'Yeah, but I stay out of the sun because I burn easily.' She'd covered up even more when her spine problems had emerged. 'And we didn't go on holidays. My parents always had a project on.'

His expression tightened. 'But you're their only child, right? Didn't they spoil you?'

She'd never been spoiled like this.

Awkwardly she undid the cord of her wrap dress. That first night it had been almost dark and since then her clothing had been loose enough to hide the unevenness of her body. It wasn't as bad as it had once been; still, for the first time in ages, she felt self-conscious. She'd never shown anyone her scar like this. Why would she when she'd seen the unveiled disappointment on her parents' faces? She glanced at him.

He was staring at her but behind those sunglasses it was impossible to tell what he was thinking. Where exactly he was looking. So she broached it directly.

'My waist looks uneven because of my spine,' she said briefly.

'I hadn't noticed.' A husky apologetic tone. 'I wasn't looking at your waist…'

He removed the sunglasses and the expression in his eyes was blatantly carnal. A surge of heat scampered across her skin because she recognised that primal expression of *want*. But now she'd pointed out her imperfection to him he blinked and his gaze slowly lowered.

Her scoliosis hadn't bothered her as much as it had bothered her parents. It was their reaction that had hurt her—their shame over something she'd not been able to control and their determination to correct it without anyone knowing. As if her deformity had to be a dreadful secret. They'd hurried her to specialists and demanded correction.

'It became obvious when I was about eleven and started growing. Initially the specialists weren't sure whether I'd need surgery but my parents pushed for it—the argument being that it would prevent it from progressing. Really, they wanted me to be perfect. I never was, of course, no matter what happened with my spine,' she said.

Her truth told, she turned so he could see the scar.

It wasn't something that *she'd* wanted to hide—it had been her mother who had wanted her to wear the loose dresses, as if her remaining asymmetry was still an embarrassment. But Rosanna had survived those months of recovery, mostly alone, and so she knew she could endure other hardships too. If anything, she was a bit proud of it—but revealing it to someone else?

That was scarier.

He was behind her now and it mattered just that little bit too much that he was quiet. But then she felt the lightest of touches on her skin as he traced her scar.

'That's a long incision,' he muttered. 'It must've been painful.'

'At the time, very.' She bent her head. Initially after the operation it had been excruciating. She didn't like to think of those first few weeks often. But not only had it stopped her curve from worsening, it had improved it a lot. Just not enough for her parents. 'My parents wanted them to do it again because they weren't happy with the outcome. But I was okay with it.'

'Does it get sore?'

'Only sometimes. Mostly it's fine.'

'It must've taken a while to recover.'

'No sports for a year. I wasn't devastated,' she admitted dryly.

He chuckled. 'No? You weren't all jolly hockey sticks?'

'I was a nerd. Enforced rest gave me time to draw.'

'Will the pregnancy cause you pain?' His voice was very husky now. 'You'll be able to take the strain of carrying two babies?'

She paused. 'When I recovered from the operation

they said childbearing should be fine in the future. I guess I should see my specialist when we get back to Sydney.'

His finger pressed a little heavier on her skin. 'We should have done that already.'

'I don't think I'm going to expand all that quickly.' She half laughed. 'And if it does get sore, it won't be anything dreadful.'

'I don't want you to be in any pain.' He lifted his hand away.

She felt the loss of that tiny contact. 'Lots of women have backache when pregnant. At least I'm used to it. And it may not even happen.' She turned to face him again. 'I'm still not perfect but it's better than it was.'

He looked down at her. She felt almost naked in front of him now but there was something in his eyes that her sad brain wanted to read as admiration.

'No one's ever perfect, Rosanna, but you're *strong*,' he said softly. 'You have a steel spine. For real.'

She smiled gently.

'If you can handle surgery like that, you can handle anything.' His hands lightly shaped each side of her waist—one side indented, the other more straight.

It didn't matter though, just the look in his eyes made her feel wanted—and his words? They filled her with a blaze of heat that was new. A *power*. He'd seen and he'd not thought any less of her, in fact he thought along the lines she'd secretly felt. That she had some grit. And now she was struggling to remember what she'd been telling him. *Why* she'd been telling him.

She drew in a steadying breath and remembered. It had been about her *parents*. Because? She felt an instinctive, self-protective need to hold him at a distance. She'd tell him everything. Anything to distract herself from the temptation he posed. Nothing would push him away more than discussion of her parents. The sooner she said it all, the sooner they could move on and he would understand why she didn't want to marry him. Why she *couldn't*. She stepped back from his touch and his hands dropped.

'You have to understand my parents excel in hyperbole and the pursuit of perfection—I got braces, and a steel rod in my spine, to make me...better, so I could be the future face of the business—it's all about appearances, right? They wanted me to be my best, not always what was best for me. Whatever I did was embellished because I wasn't ever quite good enough.' She laughed awkwardly, quickly getting through the worst. 'And I didn't want to let them down. Their work is the whole reason they married. They share a passion for design and they wanted to be the best so they teamed up. It's everything. They always held parties to show off their home—networking events really. I was shy and hid in the background and by the time I was old enough to help out they wanted me to stay out of sight until my spine had been straightened. And teeth. The freckles could be faded with make-up.'

'Didn't they see that all these things are part of what make you unique?' He frowned. 'You're stunning, Rosanna.'

She battled another blush and tried to ignore him. She'd not been fishing for compliments, she'd just been trying to explain where she came from so he'd understand why she didn't want a businesslike marriage.

'They said boarding school was to help me get past the shyness and isolation of surgery but it was more for the connections they could make with the parents there. They wanted me to make connections. Ash Castle attended, as did all the other heirs to the social empire, you know? Future leaders and all those bright young things.'

'They sent you to a school because of who attended?'

'They subscribe to the "who you know" rather than "what you know" school of success. That's what's always worked for them up until now.'

His expression stiffened. 'And that's changed since I took over. I understand their disappointment but they shouldn't have shipped corporate secrets. It was more than disloyal.'

'It was,' she agreed simply. 'The only thing I can think is that he was desperate. Success is everything to them.'

'Is it everything to you?'

'No. Not their definition of it anyway,' she said. 'I was supposed to follow them into the family business. That's why they called me Rose—because my father is known as Red. It was supposed to be a cute marketing plan for Gold Style that I couldn't live up to. I don't have the design flair, I don't have the social skills needed to sell the concepts…' She huffed out a breath. 'When I did well at school that was the one thing they could celebrate. But then they pushed too hard in that and suddenly I'm supposed to be a genius. I was put up a year because they were so pushy and told the teachers I was gifted. I had to work so hard to maintain the grades they told everyone came so easily. They were resigned to my not being in the business only if I then excelled academically. It was a relief to go to university but, honestly, even there I've not done what I "should" have. I was supposed to have been a prodigy, instead I just did my degree and then took a job as a technician because I didn't want to leave…' It had been safe there. 'But that hasn't stopped my parents telling everyone I'm a *professor*. I avoid coming back to Sydney too often so I don't have to disappoint them all over again.'

'Your value shouldn't be based on a list of achievements.'

'Says the ultimate over-achiever.'

'It was survival for me,' he said briefly. 'Do you enjoy your job?' He'd asked her that before, but now, in a way, she could answer him.

'I applied for a lectureship last month so my parents could finally be telling the truth.'

'So you're still trying to please them. Still pushing yourself along a path that's not really of your choosing.'

'I've failed though.' She shrugged. 'Didn't get the job.'

'Did you really want it?' he asked her astutely.

She sighed. 'Maybe not. Maybe I didn't really push for the projects that would've promoted me. Honestly? I was tired after striving so hard all through school to keep those grades. But it's the expectation, isn't it? To fulfil the dreams and expectations of your parents.'

She didn't live up to her potential or the expectations others had of her.

'What about your *own* dreams and expectations? If you never had to worry about money or status or what anyone thought…what would you do?'

'I don't know.' She'd never taken a breath to figure out for herself what she wanted.

'You like to grow things.'

She laughed. 'That's just a hobby.'

'That's a passion,' he corrected. 'And passion is a good thing.'

'You can't make money from plants.'

'Sure you can.' He cocked his head. 'Anyway, you don't need to make money.'

'I don't want to be dependent on you.' Her laughter faded. 'I don't want anything like my parents' marriage, where it's basically a business arrangement and the projection of their image, the look of it, is their priority.'

'We won't have that,' he said quietly. 'This isn't about the look of it. We're working together *only* in the sense of doing what's best for those babies. You're free to find fulfilment in your work, Rosanna. I'll support you in anything you want to do.'

That wasn't quite what she'd meant. Yet he made it seem as if it *would* be different—and that was tempting. He'd already shown her he could cast work aside to focus on the 'family' he wanted to build. But there was still something missing. The *heart* of it.

'Do you have any scars?' she asked, suddenly needing to push back on him in some way. 'Now I've shown you mine.'

'None on the outside,' he said.

'Nothing?' she pressed. 'Not even from some silly scrape?'

No. He was total physical perfection.

He shook his head. 'Millions underneath though.'

She regarded him warily, unsure about prying further but curiosity couldn't be contained. And he was the one who mentioned it… 'Such as?'

Leo studied her, his heart pounding. It was fair enough of her to ask. She'd opened up to him. And it was a way of distracting himself from the desire to kiss her.

'It was hard,' he finally said quietly. 'And I felt very alone.'

'Your mother must have suffered when Hugh wouldn't admit he was your father.'

'Very much so.' He hated remembering it. 'She tried for a long time to manage without asking anyone for help.'

'Where was her family?'

'They'd washed their hands of her.'

'That seems cruel.'

'Very. Unforgiving.' He nodded. He had the same fault—he'd never forgive them. 'I was about eight when she took me with her to face Hugh Castle. She'd got that desperate. He literally closed the door on us.'

'I'm sorry.'

He didn't tell Rosanna it wasn't the first time his mother had tried. Nor was it the worst thing Hugh had done to her. 'It's important to me that our children don't face any uncertainty,' he said. 'That you don't suffer anything in the way of what she suffered. I can't let that happen to you.'

'Where is she now?'

He couldn't answer for a moment. 'She passed away when I was a teenager.'

'Before…'

Everything. 'Before I had any success. Before I

proved Hugh was my father. Before I could give her any real security.'

Talking about this wasn't working. It made him want to touch her just to avoid these memories and the misery they roused. He shouldn't use Rosanna like that.

She was trembling but trying to hide it. She stepped just beyond reach each time he brushed too close—hyper aware of his proximity. As he was of hers. That kind of awareness made him wonder about her experience again. Maybe she'd been working too hard for too long and there'd not been the time. Maybe that shyness, that self-consciousness she mentioned had stopped her letting anyone get too close. But now she had no choice.

Yet she wasn't *afraid* of him, he didn't think. She'd trusted him enough to come away with him. To talk to him. But to touch him? She stepped back the very second it looked as if she was about to lean forward and kiss him. As if she were desperately stopping herself.

Maybe that was just desperately wishful thinking on his part.

'I hear what you're saying and I'm sorry for what you went through…but it isn't going to make me change my mind,' she said. 'It can't.'

He felt it as pure challenge. He shouldn't. This *wasn't* a game, there was too much precious at stake. And yet there was that electricity between them that made him want to push closer, to challenge, to make her laugh.

'Stop worrying,' he said, to himself as much as anything. 'I know it's a little complicated, but it could be worse. At least you're not my secret stepmother's illegitimate half-sister's niece or something really scandalous.'

She laughed and his spirits lightened. He liked it when she laughed. And if he didn't step away from her right now he was going to break his promises to both of them.

'Let's go explore,' he growled.

Swimming lazily, snorkelling, taking in the stunning sight of the corals beneath the water. It was a hidden garden, a whole world of beauty and wonder. It should have been the perfect distraction—absorbing them both completely. Then they walked along the shore. Even without getting in the water there was so much to observe. She often crouched, gazing at the foliage of some of the plants, watching the insects. Everywhere she looked there was something even more amazing. She couldn't help pointing things out to him as the joy of discovery overrode her usual quietness. It was lush and vital and unlike anywhere he'd ever been. He felt as if he were living in a wildlife documentary. But the most striking, fascinating creature was the angular, fiery yet pale woman alongside him. She was insightful. Yet also innocent. A pleaser who wanted more for her own children.

He wanted her to stay relaxed and satisfied. Which meant he didn't want her to worry about anything. The anger he'd felt towards her parents' betrayal faded slightly in the light of that and in what she'd told him. He was going to have to work something out when they returned to Sydney. He was going to have to fix it.

Two hours later Rosanna sat in the shade and distractedly doodled in her notebook. She couldn't help thinking about what he'd told her about his mother and his father. It would have been awful, never to have been accepted. That kind of rejection went far further than skin deep. No wonder he had that drive to win. She felt guilty for not cutting the guy some slack. He wanted to do what was right.

He was back in the pool, resting his head on his arms at the edge, the rest of him floating. She sipped sparkling water yet felt that dizzying tingle as if it were champagne. Was she drunk on the mere sight of him? His nearness? Or was it his attention—he'd stayed near her on that walk, looking at the pools she looked into, talking with her at each point. She swept her hair up into a loose ponytail to cool her neck. And now he was looking at her the way he'd looked at the fish she'd pointed out to him earlier.

'I can feel you staring at me,' she grumbled. He was making her hands shake.

'I like watching you.' He sounded amused.

'You need a hobby.'

'Why can't you be my hobby?'

She braved a look at him. 'I've no plans to be anyone's plaything.'

'That wasn't what I meant.' His mouth curved dangerously. 'But it doesn't seem like that terrible an idea.'

'Leo…'

He laughed and her world stopped. He was too gorgeous when he smiled and utterly irresistible when he laughed.

'Sorry if I've made you uncomfortable, but you fascinate me.'

She shook her head in disbelief. 'There's nothing fascinating about me. No mystery.'

'I think you're wrong about that. And I like seeing what you notice,' he added. 'You're more observant than anyone I've met. You discover the smallest things.'

'It's because I take the time to bother. Lots of people are too busy trying to talk or flirt or something.'

A smile flickered but his gaze sharpened. 'You don't like to talk? Or flirt?'

She shook her head.

'There was me thinking redheads were feisty and vivacious and full of spirited temper,' he teased.

'Not shy and awkward and basically mute?' she muttered. 'Stereotypes don't help anyone.'

'You weren't shy around me. Or awkward. Or basically mute.' He leaned closer to study her. 'That night you were the absolute opposite of that.'

She'd been different then. Because she'd lost her reason and let him do anything. Everything.

'You were different that night too,' she said. 'Because, generally, you're more serious than anyone I've ever met,' she said. 'Very focused and rigid.'

He stared at her for a second and then laughed again. 'Rigid?' He drew a breath. 'And yet around you I laugh. Often. Isn't it interesting, the devastating effect we have on each other?'

She swallowed. She didn't want to talk about the effect he had on her and she couldn't stay still with him this close. She stalked inside and chose a novel from the shelves in the lounge. She desperately needed distraction.

When she went back to the deck she saw Leo in the distance. He'd taken himself for a run. It was almost an hour before he returned, slick with sweat and effort. He briefly stood beneath the outdoor shower and it took every ounce of her willpower not to drool at the display. Then the infuriating, stunning man dived back into the pool. Rosanna tried to read the novel.

'Do you even *know* how to relax?' Rosanna glared at him when he finally paused for breath.

'By relax you mean lie about and do nothing?' He shook his head, spraying droplets of water as he laughed. 'That's not how I relax.'

'I'm lying about doing nothing because I'm *not* doing nothing. I'm reading. Plus I'm growing babies. Tell me how *you* supposedly relax, then. At the office?'

'I enjoy it. It's exhilarating. There's always some new challenge.'

And she'd deprived him of that challenge by daring him to take a holiday. She had the horrible feeling *she'd* become his new challenge.

Surely him busy working would be better than him being fully focused on her? He'd become even more of a temptation with his attention. When he laughed it was as if the biggest fireworks display lit up the dark sky. Brilliance cascaded from him and enveloped her in its spillover, lighting her up. She needed him back on his conference calls or whatever. Not on her.

She couldn't concentrate on the damn book.

CHAPTER ELEVEN

LEO FLOATED, SHOCKED by his uncontrolled thoughts. He was actually jealous of the attention she was giving a *book*. But he wanted her to look at him instead. He wanted her to talk to him some more. To lead him on another stroll along the beach and point out small insects no one else would even spot. He'd had to take himself for a run to burn some of the insane sexual energy he was struggling to contain.

He ought to be worrying about work. About the deluge of emails probably overflowing in his inbox. Instead he was focused entirely on Rosanna. Right now, all he wanted to see was that heat in her eyes that he'd seen that night all those weeks ago. But the uncertainty and shyness she'd shown since being here? That had made him think. What she'd told him of her upbringing—she'd spent long tracts of time alone when recovering, she was a dreamer, not a party creature. She'd liked to draw and read books. Now the creeping suspicion built into a whisper of certainty. She wasn't just shy, she was *inexperienced*. Not just sexually but with emotional intimacy too. In that last the pair of them were alike.

She finally turned the page of her book. Now he thought about it, she was making surprisingly slow progress with it given how much time she'd had her nose in it. He cocked his head as another suspicion entered his mind. Was she even reading it?

'What's it about?' he called to her from the pool.

'Hmm?'

'The book. What's it about?'

'Oh…um…' She flicked to the back.

'No, don't read me the blurb,' he teased. 'You tell me.'

She sighed. 'I don't know. I can't get into it.'

Yet she'd been staring at it so studiously for ages. Which meant she couldn't concentrate on anything either.

It more than tickled him. It gave him hope.

The way their fingers brushed when he handed her a glass of sparkling water. The way his arm pressed against hers when they were seated together in the small boat when out exploring. The way he focused on the small things she pointed out to him. The way his gaze lingered on her when she walked past him. Every instance was so tiny yet so hot and so intense. And every one felt as though it was leading her to something that was inevitable. The chemistry was drawing her closer and closer to him. She shivered with need for more of his touch. It was as if she'd succumbed to an illness and there was only one cure. The only thing that saved her from total humiliation was that he seemed to feel it too.

'Dance with me,' he invited after they'd eaten a sumptuous dinner of fresh baked fish and verdant salad.

She eyed him warily.

'Please,' he added.

It was an echo of that first night together. When they'd danced another way entirely.

'I don't dance.'

'Nor do I,' he said simply. 'But I'm tempted to now.'

A warm spurt of amusement trickled through her. She liked his honesty with her. 'Are we going to stand on each other's feet, then?'

His expression warmed. 'We have better rhythm with each other than that, as well you know, Ms Gold. I think we can do okay.'

He picked up the remote for the entertainment unit. A second later music floated through the hidden speakers. He had that unpractised, uneven smile that she found irresistible. He knew the effect he had on her, didn't he? She studied him, saw the intent in his eyes as he approached her.

'Do you think it's wise?' she muttered.

'Are you afraid I might overstep the boundaries?'

She shook her head. She wasn't afraid of *him* but of herself. 'No. You can tell me over and over that work is wonderful, but it is still *work* and there must have been times when you've wanted to do something else but you haven't let yourself,' she said. 'Which makes you a master of self-control. So I think *not* overstepping will be very easy for you.'

Impossibly his gaze intensified. 'I guess the difference is I don't want to deny myself the pleasure to be had with *you*. I don't want to waste all that effort and energy when it could be used on something so much better.'

From just his words another blush burned through her. It wasn't fair. He knew she couldn't resist his touch. She racked her brains with increasing desperation for some way to put a barrier between them—make him turn away from her.

'You know I kissed your half-brother,' she muttered huskily.

'My half-brother has kissed most of the women your age in the whole damned country, as far as I can tell,' he replied lazily.

He didn't seem jealous at all. Now she felt miffed because the thought of Leo kissing another woman made *her* want to stab something.

'Don't forget to dance, Rosanna,' he chided softly, that smile audible now.

She closed her eyes and felt him draw her closer.

'Rumour has it Ash is a renowned lover,' Leo muttered idly. 'What did you think?'

She stilled and glared up at him.

He stopped moving too. 'You just said you kissed him.' His tone was all innocence yet there was sharpness in his eyes. Maybe she'd been wrong about that lack of jealousy?

'That was *all*,' she said.

'Oh?' Leo asked, still with that dispassionate tone, yet the angularity of his features tightened. 'Why not everything else? I mean, his reputation is—'

'I didn't want to,' she mumbled, completely regretting ever mentioning it. The truth was Ash hadn't wanted to sleep with her either.

'And yet with *me*,' Leo said quietly, 'a complete stranger, you wanted everything.' He pressed her waist closer against his. 'You, who—as far as I can tell—hasn't really dated anyone, let me have you in almost an instant.'

She suddenly felt his tension—he held his big body in check but he was *wired*.

Fraught, she was vulnerable and exposed. 'That's not something worth discussing.'

'I think it is. I'd like to know why.' He gazed into her eyes. 'Or are you not up to trusting me yet?'

'I do trust you,' she said. Truthfully she always had.

'Then tell me why you let me touch you that night.'

The flush of heat over her body was appalling. She didn't really know why Leo was the only one to press her buttons—only that once he'd pressed them there'd been no off switch. 'I think I was tired,' she mumbled.

'Tired?' He chuckled. 'No.'

'Leo…' A wall of heat enveloped her.

'It's okay.' He cupped her cheek, feeling for himself the way her skin scalded. 'At the risk of coming off like a complete jerk, I'm pleased I'm your only lover, Rosanna,' he said huskily. 'That I'm the only one to have entered your body. The only one who knows how hot you truly run. How silken and snug your gorgeous body is. The only one who's heard those little moans you can't hold back because you're about to come.'

She was appalled that he'd guessed her secret and appalled at the heat washing through her now—it was so intense, so sudden, that she was almost about to come again now. His touch tossed her back into the heated swirl of bliss that only he'd summoned within her.

'Stop it,' she mumbled.

But she didn't mean it. She wanted more—she ached

for that easy obliteration of every damn thought, care, worry…all burned in the heat of ecstasy that he could give. She could feel the tension within him. The arousal. It mirrored her own. She was so close to kissing him.

It was overwhelming. And frightening. Because everything was different now. This wasn't one magic moment, one night that could be kept a secret for always. They had complications to deal with. But she couldn't back away from him the way she knew she ought to. She couldn't cope with the intensity of his magnetism. Why was this so immense? Maybe it was the pregnancy hormones making her so sensitive—was that a thing? Or was it a biological urge to cling to the nearest big, strong male because she was pregnant…a primitive need to seek security? Leo was big and strong and powerful. He was also the most handsome man she'd ever laid eyes on. He was also holding her in a way that made her feel *everything*.

'I'm right, aren't I?' he added almost hoarsely.

She turned her head slightly. 'It shouldn't matter.'

'But it does. To you. To me. What's going on, Rosanna?' He shook her gently. 'You didn't think that was something I should've known?'

'How could I tell you?' She looked up at him, her heart burning. 'I didn't think it would matter. You were very courteous. Very…careful to ensure I was having a good time.'

His hold on her tightened. 'I could've made it better,' he growled.

Rosanna stared. As if that were even possible?

His dimple suddenly appeared and the indigo in his eyes lit. 'You don't think it could've been better?'

She shouldn't admit anything more. This was so mortifying. Yet it didn't seem to matter that he knew—and so, yet more of the truth slipped out. 'It was like a dream to me.'

One that had devastatingly real consequences. But now he smiled at her. A full, devastating, gorgeous smile that rendered her spellbound. She was utterly entranced and she couldn't regret that night. Not then, not now, not ever. Not even though they now faced a complicated future because of it. She had to get hold of herself to be able to *think*. Summoning her last speck of resistance, she pushed him. He immediately stepped back.

'What are you doing?' he asked as she raced indoors.

'Getting your phone for you,' she muttered.

'Why?' He stood in the doorway. 'I don't want it.'

He began to laugh as he watched her furiously stabbing the numbers on the hotel safe.

'Sure you do,' she argued. 'You want it. You've been missing it. Aching for it. I bet your fingers are itching.'

'My fingers *are* itching,' he conceded. 'But not to touch my phone.'

'Stop it.' She all but begged him.

His smile was slow and so infuriating and a glint that reeked of smug satisfaction lit his beautiful eyes. 'You can't handle this. You're looking to take me out,' he said. 'I'm winning.'

He was *not* winning. She finally got the safe open. Ignoring her own phone, she snatched up his and turned to face him, holding it in front of her like the temptation she knew it was.

'Rosanna.' His voice was low and gravelly but it wasn't a warning.

There was delight in his eyes and it fired a playfulness within her. She would catch him out, wouldn't she? Distract him with the thing most important to him.

'Don't you want to come nearer?' she teased him.

'I think it's best if I don't answer that.'

He remained in the doorway. Didn't venture so much as a step closer. Which meant she had to move closer to him again.

She pressed the button to light up the screen and held it up before her like a weapon. 'Look at all those notifications. All those emails. Missed calls and everything.'

'Rosanna...' The gleam in his eye turned feral with the promise of retribution.

A low burn deep in her belly, a strength coiling within her. A hunger. 'Take it, Leo,' she tempted him with a soft sultry tone. 'You know you want to.'

She stopped walking, holding the phone so he could just reach it—but not the rest of her.

'Oh, I know exactly what I want.' He grabbed the phone but didn't so much as glance at the screen before turning to throw it away. It whipped through the air and splashed into the pool behind him.

'What?' Rosanna shrieked and ran past him to the edge of the water. 'What did you just do?'

She stared at the spot where the phone had splashed into the pool and immediately sunk. Then she slowly turned and stared at him.

'You did not do that. You did *not* just do that.' She was stunned. That was him, wasn't it? A man of action. Not passive. She needed to be more like him in that respect and now anticipation scalded her insides. 'Aren't you going to go in and get it? It'll be ruined.'

He had the widest, wildest smile. And she couldn't cope—nor could she tear her gaze from him and that ferociously playful expression in his eyes. His *phone* was at the bottom of the pool and he was…smiling?

'It's waterproof, right?' she checked. 'It's new and fancy and waterproof.'

'Don't know. Don't care.' He stepped towards her. 'But what's very interesting is that you're so keen for me to be distracted by something other than *you*.' He stopped the merest inch away from her and whispered, 'Can't you cope with my attention, Rosanna?'

Her heart pounded as sensual energy scurried around her body. She was so close to surrender and he knew it.

'Don't be mean,' she breathed.

'I'm not being mean, I'm being *honest*. Why don't you give it a go? You might find it a relief.'

She gazed, lost in his eyes.

His *attention* terrified her. She wasn't entirely sure what she was afraid of…getting hurt? In this situation, hurt was inevitable. They were tied to each other for the rest of their lives. They were having children together. That didn't mean they were going to be together. But they'd be connected. Their lives intertwined—through custody arrangement, meeting for handovers, both attending school concerts. It saddened her—which she knew was stupid. Because all of that could be okay. People handled that just fine all the world over. And from far worse situations. At least she actually liked him. But *that* was the problem, wasn't it? And from where her fear actually sprang was that she would want more. Always more. And he didn't want to give it to her. He'd already said, hadn't he? That once he had enough of something, he didn't want it any more.

But at least she'd have had this.

Finally, she appreciated that this might be her one chance. She was doing herself a disservice by denying herself, wasn't she?

'Are *your* fingers itching, sweetheart?' He laughed softly. 'Shall I tell you again?' he tempted softly. 'How badly mine are? How much I ache to touch you properly again?'

She closed her eyes as he stepped closer still, that one last pace until he was pressed against her. His arm went around her waist, holding her close. She refused to listen. Refused to feel.

'You have another phone, right?' she muttered, her eyes still closed, desperately fixating on the phone horror in a final last attempt. 'A secret one hidden in your bag somewhere. You've probably been working while I've been asleep.'

'Oh, Rosanna.' His breath gently stirred the hair at her temple. 'What a highly active imagination you've got. I'm absolutely innocent of all those charges. I *have* been awake though, with my imagination working overtime.'

And he'd needed to dip in that cool water in the middle of the night. She'd seen him.

'Are you going to open your eyes and look at me?' he asked.

The tiredness that had pervaded her mind and limbs over these last two weeks evaporated. It was as if a mist lifted from her and revealed a deep well of energy that wanted to be burned in one way only. Her weak mind presented her with all kinds of temptations. Suddenly she didn't know why she'd felt such a strong need to resist him. Was she mad? Why wouldn't she want to experience this again? It would all be fine. As she opened her eyes he smiled. It wasn't full of satisfaction. It was full of genuine reassurance.

'You look so serious.' He touched her cheek again.

Her lips were horribly dry, her throat tight. 'That's usually you.'

'What's holding you back?' he asked.

The last scrap of truth escaped. 'Because I'm not good at this.' Being intimate in any way with anyone.

'You're good at it with me.'

Heat flushed through her. It scared her how much he affected her.

He cupped her face in both his hands. 'It's just sex, sweetheart.'

She badly wanted to believe that but, considering how overwhelming she found him...

'It won't complicate things any more than they already are,' he promised. 'And it might help us both think more clearly.'

'You can't think clearly either?' she asked. Because thoughts and doubts and dreams endlessly swirled in total confusion in her mind.

'You've been the only thing on my mind for months.'

His admission melted her. In the end there was only the certainty of feeling and the simplicity of truth. She wanted him. She wanted this.

'Kiss me.' Her lips were dry, her skin stretched tight,

she was sure he ought to be able to hear the hum in her blood.

'Rosanna?' A broken check for reassurance.

'Please.'

The second he touched his lips to hers she was incinerated by the intensity of their connection. The determination on his face ought to have terrified her. Instead she felt a welcome relief, a burgeoning satisfaction of her own because she understood he intended to please her *entirely.*

He set out to shatter her into total oblivion. She relished being that challenge for him. As he was hers. He advanced on her with nothing but success in his mind. The mantle of respectability was gone, revealing raw lust. The desire to give and take pleasure—the thing one and the same. As inexperienced as she was, she knew there was something about her that pushed his buttons. And as temporary as it might be, there was no denying it now.

'You're so bloody beautiful.'

'You say that as if it's a bad thing.'

'You bewitch me. You did that night. A sprite in amongst the greenery. Like a garden nymph, stealing what she wanted.'

'You still think I'm a thief?'

'I know you are.' He touched her. 'Dangerous and beautiful and utterly irresistible.'

'I'm not dangerous.'

'Oh, but you are *so* dangerous to my peace of mind.' His expression tightened.

None of her concerns mattered any more. The fight to resist him faded. The decisions of their future were forgotten. Because he was here and he was touching her and there was only now. Lost in his kiss, she reached for him, sliding his tee up his flat abs, exposing his body to her hungry eyes, her ravenous touch.

'Not so fast. Last time was fast. This time...' he breathed out '...slow.'

But she needed him now. She needed this awful ache to be eased. She needed that hit of pleasure unlike anything she'd known. Now she'd decided—*surrendered*— there could be no slowing down, no stopping.

He laughed beneath his breath and stopped her by simply picking her up and carrying her to the bed where he slowly but deftly peeled back her bikini.

'Your skin is so freaking amazing,' he growled.

She smiled, marvelling in the pleasure of him finding her so attractive. It might only be chemistry, but it was fierce and strong and so very real. And he took delight in tormenting her—so slowly, until she was literally screaming with her need for completion. She cried out as he thrust home. Finally she felt the fullness she'd craved for weeks. His hands tightened beneath her, holding her closer as he pushed harder and deeper. And that sweet relief was underpinned by the ache of need. Every layer peeled away to reveal the only thing that really mattered. He didn't need to gloat. He was more serious than that. She saw the determination anew in his eyes.

'I've missed you.' He gazed into her eyes, triumph blazing in his own.

It mirrored the satisfaction flowing through her.

Slowly he moved and kissed her again as he did. A soul-destroying kiss that broke down any defence she'd thought she might be able to rebuild, leaving her raw and vulnerable to him—an open book of emotion for him to devour.

So it was far too late when she realised that he was going to take it *all*.

CHAPTER TWELVE

LEO SAT ON the deck, appreciating the view in a way that was wholly new to him. Rosanna was paddling in the shallows, investigating little fish, noticing the smallest of things as she took those few extra seconds to truly observe. She silently saw so much—feeling deeply, appreciating. He found himself more aware as a result, keen to spot something ahead of her so he could draw her attention to it. In that way, she'd opened up his world. So now he noticed the little lizard sunning itself near his foot. Bright eyes, alert, watching him. He couldn't resist smiling at it and broke off a bit of his bacon sandwich to toss to it.

He ought to be satisfied yet it felt as if a blade were still pressed upon his throat. A sense of threat remained, pushing him to secure more. Physical—sexual—intimacy was easy to achieve. He liked discovering what made her sigh or cry for relief, what make her shake, what made her laugh. But he felt driven to discover *more*. What she'd told him about her life—he wanted to know more of what she wanted. How she felt. It was weird to be so curious about someone. He tossed another piece of the meat to the lizard.

'You've found a friend?' She waded towards him.

'Maybe.'

'Do you have many others?' she asked lightly.

It soothed him that she was curious about him too.

He nodded. 'Ash.'

His half-brother was the closest he had to any kind of best friend. But now, even though he knew his half-brother had chased off to another country after some woman…the thought of him having history with Rosanna burned. It shouldn't matter at all. For a while it *hadn't*. Yet now he couldn't stop himself asking. 'What really happened between you two?'

Colour washed over her skin. He didn't read anything into her blush. It was almost standard when he asked her something. 'You said you'd kissed him…'

'You really want to know?'

Leo glanced away and then back at her. 'It's just that it's not like him to walk away from a woman without…'

Rosanna sat beside him. 'I was hardly a woman at the time.'

Leo frowned. 'When was it?'

'After my surgery.' She swallowed. 'I didn't just have to return to school, but move to a new one miles away from my home. I'd been in hospital, then had several months alone in recovery and, honestly, I just wanted to stay at home for a while and be in one that wasn't being redecorated yet again. But my parents were ready to move onto their next project and decided it was "better" if I was away at boarding school. They said it would give me the stability I'd been asking them for. Plus now I was all fixed up, it was time for me to acquire the social skills they said I needed.'

'Social skills?'

'To cultivate beneficial relationships. It's how they operate, remember?' She rolled her eyes. 'Because they'd talked me up academically, the school did as they asked and put me in a higher grade so I was by far the youngest student in the class. I didn't know anyone, I felt awkward and a huge amount of pressure to maintain my scores.' She bent her head. 'I didn't know it at the time, but my mother had asked Ash's mother to get him to keep an eye out for me.'

'And did he?'

She nodded. 'He hung out with me more than most, and we went out a couple of times. Then he asked me to be his date to the senior dance. It made me instantly popular and, fool that I was, I thought I could do what my parents wanted. Learn how to use a relationship to get ahead in life.' She smiled sadly. 'Ash had an awful lot of sway over people, so it was ideal, right?'

Leo had a bad feeling hearing the bitterness in her tone. 'What happened?'

'The dance didn't go so well,' she muttered. 'He had a…moment with a couple of other girls and it was videoed.'

'A moment?' Leo groaned; he could well imagine the sort of 'moment' she meant. 'He humiliated you.'

'Of course, I felt hurt when I first saw the clip. And that my classmates took such delight in publicly playing it to me. It went viral and became the school's most notorious event.'

'I bet,' Leo murmured.

That would've been enough to send *any* sensitive

young woman into a cave for a while. And Rosanna was sensitive.

'But honestly?' She straightened a little to look at him. 'With the benefit of a few years, I can look back on it now and realise a part of me felt relieved. I knew he wasn't into me in that way. And I wasn't into him. It ended all that pressure. Not that *he* put that on me at all. When I think about it now, he was actually lovely.'

'Ash Castle, *lovely*?' Leo joked dryly but his chest had tightened—what *pressure*? Did she mean from her parents?

'Back then he had so much going on and we didn't know the extent. He was trying to be kind but he just couldn't resist, I guess. He was having an awful time and I suppose he needed an escape. I was embarrassed, but I wasn't *devastated* by him getting off with two other girls when he was supposed to be on a date with me. Later I found out he'd only asked me because his mother had told him to. She was so unwell, he'd have done anything for her. Honestly, it was more mortifying that *my* mother had tried to sort out my social life for me by talking to his mother in the first place.'

'Oh.' Leo nodded, his suspicions confirmed. 'Your parents again, huh?'

'They were furious with me.'

'You? He was the one who got filmed.'

'And he was disciplined and never returned to school. Then his mother died. It must have been horrendous.' She drew in a deep breath. 'Meanwhile my parents said I obviously hadn't been a good girlfriend if I hadn't kept his interest. I hadn't done my job or whatever...'

'They blamed you?' Outrage built in his chest. 'What did they want you to *do*, exactly?'

'Better,' she said simply. 'But I don't think it's in me. Not to "work" relationships like that.'

His curiosity bit—she'd been so *abandoned* with him that night, yet he knew she'd been inexperienced. Maybe not just sexually. 'And you haven't dated anyone since?'

Her lashes lifted, revealing shy amusement in her pale blue eyes. 'You think I'm some sort of exotic species?'

'Like some of those creatures on the reef?' He shrugged. 'Perhaps.'

Honestly, he didn't know what to make of her. She was shy yet warm once he'd got past her quiet barrier. She could be clinically detached, yet compassionate and loyal. Maybe she was too shy to ask someone, but he couldn't believe no other guys had ever asked *her* out.

'After the incident with Ash I suppose I was put off for a bit,' she admitted. 'I certainly wasn't about to date anyone at school again. Nor in my class at uni. And I'm *never* going to date anyone I work with.'

Leo half smiled. So now she had a bunch of rules as to who she could or couldn't date? 'Sounds like you know what you don't want.'

'Not some society stud like Ash, that's for sure.'

Right—which also might rule him out. 'No colleagues, no one your parents would approve of?' He worked it through. 'Which makes it hard to find anyone you could say *yes* to.'

She glanced away and then back at him. His skin

tightened. It had taken only seconds for her to say yes to him.

'You thought I was a security guard,' he mused. Not a colleague. Not a threat. 'Would your parents disapprove?' Had it been rebellion?

'No, it wasn't that…' She trailed off and that colour swept into her cheeks again.

'Then what?'

'I just… You were…'

'I was just what?' Something hot and fierce swirled in his blood. A ridiculous preening inside pushed him to ask why. 'What was different about me?'

'Chemistry, I guess?'

For a second he was ridiculously pleased. Then it was as if the tide of satisfaction receded and left emptiness. Because she hadn't wanted more at the time. She'd not asked for his name or number. She'd not wanted to seek him out again. He gazed at her and for the first time in his life wished that he could read minds. Never had it mattered what anyone thought of him before. But he wanted to understand why she'd walked away so easily. Because it niggled. Was it because she'd been afraid of his reaction if they'd seen each other fully naked? If he'd seen her scar and reacted in a way that made her think she wasn't good enough for him or anyone? He hated that her parents had put that on her. She was *amazing*— strong and brave. She'd been so that night with him.

That colour built in her cheeks as the silence grew.

Yet he knew she wanted him now. That he'd pleased her. He was about to do it again—was suddenly determined to do it even *more*.

'I didn't know who you were or anything about you,'

she said softly, her colour high. 'You just…swept me away.'

'Maybe that meant that with me you could relax enough to let go,' he said gruffly. 'There was no expectation. No perfect performance required for once. In your mind it didn't matter at all. And so…you could relax.'

'You think?' An expression he couldn't quite read flashed on her face. 'Damn, I should have hooked up with a total stranger sooner.'

No. No other strangers. No other guys. He almost roared it as a fierce bolt of possessiveness tore through him before he recognised the teasing note in her voice.

He scooped her up and carried her back to the big bed they'd left only an hour ago and set about sweeping her away again and again. He kissed every inch, taking care to caress her spine. Not just to tease, but to worship every sweet inch of her until neither of them could move. Even then he watched her, still wishing he could read her mind.

She studied the edge of the cotton sheet that lightly covered her, obviously trying not to blush. Failing as usual. 'Why don't *you* sleep with the billions of women who fling themselves at you on a daily basis?'

He laughed at her exaggeration. 'There aren't billions.'

Her kiss-crushed lips pouted. 'Oh, come on, there's at least five a day. I saw three at the airport on our way here. You can't have failed to see how they looked at you.'

He hadn't noticed any. 'I was too busy watching you.'

She bit her lip but the little laugh escaped regardless. 'Smooth. But not necessary. I'm already back in your bed and you've had your way with me twice this morning already.'

It hadn't been a line. It had been simple truth.

She gazed right into his eyes. 'I'm serious. Why aren't you a player? You could be if you wanted to.'

'Most of the time I'm so consumed by work I don't realise where the day has gone,' he answered as honestly as he could. 'I'm absorbed in it.'

'That's the thing that matters to you most?'

'It always has been.' At least since his mother had passed.

'You're that disciplined?'

He saw it not as discipline, but necessity. Since his mother had died it had been the only thing that mattered—work was the one way to make himself a success, to force Hugh Castle to face him, and the impetus behind his need to make something more of that man's empire than Hugh himself had ever made of it That had been everything until recently, when he'd been consumed by thoughts of Rosanna—which in itself was shockingly unnerving. The sooner they agreed their future, the sooner he would return to his usual focused state. Surely now she'd see how much sense it made for them to marry. They had chemistry, they were building a friendship. This didn't need to be that complicated.

But now she studied him in the way she did those unusual plants she was interested in—with that focused curiosity. 'You don't wake in the small hours of the morning and overthink all your most personal things?' She wrinkled her nose. 'Not ever?'

At that he smiled. 'I wake in the small hours and

overthink *work*.' But that wasn't entirely true. There were things that came to him then that he hated. 'I never wanted to be like him. Like Hugh.'

'In what way?'

'In his greed. In his cheating.' He sighed. 'I know Ash used to play the field, but he was upfront about it,' Leo said. 'Women knew where they stood with him. But I didn't want any of that complication in my life. I never wanted to make promises I couldn't keep.' He gazed at her sombrely.

'So why did you play that night with me?'

He still didn't rightly know. 'That night had been the culmination of a hard year's work. Stepping in to take over Castle Holdings. There were times I didn't think I was going to make it and I wanted to nail it.'

'To prove to the world you could be as successful as Hugh?'

There was a shadow in her expression that he didn't understand. 'You think that's stupid?'

'No.' She sat up and wrapped herself in the sheet. 'I don't blame you for wanting to better him. I would too. So you were in a celebratory mood.'

Oddly he hadn't been. He'd been tired and a bit deflated. 'It wasn't normal for me to do that either.'

She glanced at him again. 'You wanted an escape.'

'I was stunned, to be honest. I couldn't believe what had possessed me. I suddenly realised I had a roomful of people downstairs waiting on me.' He laughed a little. 'Maybe it's as you said, just chemistry. We're a perfect compound, compatible in the most fundamental of ways.'

'Is that enough for you?' She looked back at the edge of the sheet. 'You truly don't believe in love?'

He didn't know how to answer without offending her.

She lifted her head and gazed at him, her eyes soft with an emotion he didn't want to analyse. 'You don't think that one day you might meet someone and there'll be something so much more? I wouldn't want to be in the way of that happening for you.'

More?

'That's not going to happen, Rosanna.'

Maybe he should have appreciated her thoughtfulness. Instead her solicitude engendered a flash of anger. He didn't want her concern for his well-being. He was just fine. *This* was all he wanted—a straightforward fix to the situation they were in. This, just as it was, would be a good deal for them both. Companionship, good sex, security.

Or maybe she didn't think it was? Maybe she didn't realise that sex didn't get any better than it was between them… Or maybe, he realised with a hit of discomfort, she wouldn't want *him* being in the way of that happening for *her* either. She wasn't a cool-headed scientist. She had a *romantic* streak.

He couldn't deliver on that. But for what it was worth, he wanted her more than he'd ever wanted a woman and that hunger wasn't easing any. His anger built. So did his determination to get her to agree. It seemed more imperative than ever that he secure this damn deal. He could give her things no other man in her life could.

'No?' Rosanna was lost in the gleaming passion in his eyes. In the growing fervour she'd not seen in him before.

She knew he didn't have random one-night stands,

but he didn't understand that for her it hadn't been about the occasion, but the person. It had been about *him*. And she'd felt a little hit to her heart that it hadn't been she who had overwhelmed his control, it had been circumstance causing him to act the way he had that night with her. Of course, that was right. She supposed any woman who'd appeared on the terrace at that time could've ended up in his embrace, the recipient of his attentions.

'Then how lucky for me to have been the one to stumble across your path that night, huh?' she couldn't resist pointing out a little bitterly.

Something snapped in his expression. 'That night you turned up and *you* were the one I couldn't resist. I wanted to forget everything. Who I was. Where I was. What I should or shouldn't have been doing. I just watched you and I wanted you. Just as I want you again now.'

He wasn't slow that time. But the time after? That was when her last little flicker of doubt and disappointment melted. His touch was an achingly sweet relief.

Now she could luxuriate in the week they had left here. In the stillness of their surroundings there was nothing to steal any of their attention away—only the two of them alone in paradise. And when he kissed her she lost all capacity to think or to worry. She liked losing herself in his arms and becoming this creature who only felt good things. Now she satisfied the curiosity and hunger that had held her in thrall for all these weeks. She could expunge those regrets of what she'd not done sooner by doing it all now. Take her time. Take all he had to offer. In this warmth, the gentle breeze, shaded from the burning brilliance of the sun, she fully understood the delight of desire.

'This is something to build on,' he said huskily, hours later. 'I can support you, Rosanna. You can trust me.'

And when he gazed down at her, the epitome of beauty in the world around him shone and she couldn't think beyond him any more.

'Just marry me,' he tempted. 'You know we can make this work.'

That was the thing, it didn't feel like work at all. He offered her a perfect, problem-free paradise. That rough stubble on his face, the tan on his skin, the smile in his eyes, the damn dimple... He made everything seem so easy, tempting her with the promise of happiness and laughter. The off-beat pulse of panic in her blood was drowned by the heat he stirred within her and Rosanna ignored the warning strike against her ribcage.

'Yes.'

CHAPTER THIRTEEN

A FEW DAYS slid by in a mixture of laziness and activity. They snorkelled on the reef entranced by turtles, corals and fish, walked along the sand, boated to cays and other islands. Laughed about little things. He shared in her delight in finding beauty on the reef. It had been the perfect place to bring her. And each afternoon he took her back to bed after lunch, so through the hottest point of the day he was shrouded with her beneath billowing cool cotton sheets. Until there wasn't a part of her he hadn't touched and tasted ten times over.

It still wasn't enough. He was still hungry for her. He'd made a point of indulging her in every act of intimacy, teaching her just how sensitive some parts of her body could be, showing her how the peak of pleasure, a white-hot orgasm, could be achieved in a myriad ways. Then sustained. Then achieved again. Yet still there was more. There was a depth to this connection between them—a profound intimacy in the way she straddled his lap and held him locked tight into her body. He teased her, talking to her, delighting in making her unable to answer coherently. Breathless and hot and restless and so playful—teasing her, pleasuring her, making her ignite. He adored the way she flushed and responded and flipped it all against him. And still he felt a near constant ache for her.

He *should* be fast asleep. He'd already got the win, he should be enjoying the winner's spoils. She was going to marry him. There was nothing to worry about. But here he was, lying awake since the middle of the night until dawn. Overthinking. And for once it wasn't about work. It should be. He'd been out of touch for days. But instead he was worried about Rosanna's agreement. Oddly he now felt her arguments against marriage as a warning he'd not heeded. The responsibility of her happiness haunted him. He wasn't sure he could shoulder it. Here—on holiday—it was easy enough. But ordinarily he wasn't on holiday. He worked. He *needed* to work. His employees depended on him and it was the only thing he'd done for so long. The only thing he really knew how to do. What made him ever think he could be a husband and father? He killed houseplants. He'd never had pets. His children deserved a better parent than he'd ever be. Rosanna deserved a better partner.

He got up, pacing through to the lounge to grab a cool drink and clear his head.

He didn't discuss his father with anyone. Not even Ash. But he'd found himself wanting to explain to Rosanna that he'd never wanted to be the lying cheat Hugh Castle had been. To never take advantage of women—or anyone—in that way or any other. His father had been a controlling, unrelenting bastard. Leo wanted to be better than that and wanted her to know that she could trust him.

Which meant he needed to fix things with *her* parents. They'd wanted her to make a match with Ash Castle all those years ago and now they had to deal with him, the man who'd cancelled their company's contracts. But for Rosanna's peace of mind he was compelled to take action. He could send a message from his watch. She'd never know and if she did she wouldn't mind. He didn't want her experiencing any of the bitterness he'd felt with his father's rejection and no further pressure of difficulties with her parents. That didn't mean he'd forgiven them. There'd be rules and he'd make it clear they weren't to upset or pressure Rosanna in *any* way. It only took a moment to message his assistant but as he returned his watch to the safe he knocked Rosanna's phone. The screen lit up and he saw there were a number of missed notifications. The most recent message was displayed in full.

Ro, crisis at the flat. There's been a flood. Where are you? Call urgently.

The implications took a second to sink in. Then anxiety spiked. All her belongings—her plants, notebooks, weird fish…

He glanced in the doorway to their bedroom. She was fast asleep but he knew she'd worry. He could find out more about the situation first before telling her.

Quietly he walked to the office of the private resort, glad the sun was rising and it wasn't too shockingly early to phone people; glad he had something concrete to focus his worry on. Because there was an unusual amount of anxiety building within—rendering him unable to rest, unable to be easy and just enjoy this. It was stupid—hadn't he achieved exactly what he'd wanted?

She'd said *yes*. To *marriage*.

Only he wasn't sure it was right. Now he questioned whether pushing the proposal had been wise. Having her so close beside him for so long—for ever? Suddenly he felt keenly aware that she was precious—fragile really. And he didn't want to crush her. He didn't want to screw this up.

He stabbed the buttons on the office phone—avoiding the damned inner anxiety by focusing on her real issue. It turned out a water pipe had burst in the flat above her and leaked through and everything was sodden. He thought again of the things she'd put so much effort into. She didn't need the heartache of sorting this out. He could get the clean-up under way and she could have another day without knowing until the worst had been fixed up. He'd get professionals in and it could be sorted by the time they returned. He'd save her all that stress.

'You're very serious this morning.' Rosanna smiled as they returned to the villa after a couple hours out on a double kayak.

He'd been wondering how the clean-up was going. Was itching to put in a call to check. And he realised he didn't want to lie to her. 'There was a flood at your flat,' he muttered.

Her eyes widened. 'What?'

'The unit upstairs had a burst pipe. The occupant was away for the weekend as well, so no one noticed until it started coming out of your front door.'

'What?' A frown crashed on her brows. 'How do

you know?' She folded her arms and glared at him. 'So you've been using your phone.'

'No, that's wrecked from the water. I saw the message on yours when I went to get my watch from the safe.'

'When was that?'

'Early this morning.' He saw she wasn't happy and tried to explain more. 'You were fast asleep. It was easy to arrange a clean-up.'

'That's why you've been distracted.' Her frown didn't lessen. 'When were you going to tell me?'

He didn't know. 'You don't need stress at the moment. You've got enough on.'

'So you thought you'd fix it?'

'That seemed…like an idea.' He watched her warily because now she stomped inside the villa.

She whirled on the top step to face him. 'Is this what it's going to be like?'

His defensiveness rose. Like *what*? 'I just thought—'

'That you knew what was best for me.' She glared down at him. 'That you could make decisions on my behalf. For what was best for *you*.'

'Not for me. I did it for you.'

'Really? I don't need you to do that. I'm not incompetent. Or incapable. Or that useless.'

'I thought I was doing something *helpful*.' He'd been concerned for her welfare. For the health of the babies. Was that so awful of him?

'What did you think might happen if you told me before you fixed it?'

'I don't know,' he growled. 'You've been tired. I just…'

'Do you really think I'm that fragile?' She paused, something flickering in her eyes. 'You said I was strong.'

And she was. He'd just wanted to shelter her from unnecessary stress. He'd wanted to fix it for her.

'I'm not just another thing you're *responsible* for, Leo,' she said when he didn't respond. 'I need you to include me, not decide things unilaterally.'

'That wasn't what I intended.' He growled. 'I wanted to protect you.'

She paused. 'Why?' She came down from the top step so she stood eye to eye with him. 'From what?'

'I don't know,' he snapped. 'But you're vulnerable.'

'I'm *pregnant,* not incapacitated.'

And he'd never felt as frustrated. 'Look, I'm sorry but I can't risk—' He rubbed his forehead and smothered a growl. 'Life is precious, Rosanna. I've failed before. I can't do it again.'

'Failed in what way?'

He froze.

'Failed *who*, Leo?'

He stared at her. The anger was gone from her face—the flash flood of colour had receded and left her paler than usual.

'Leo?'

She was strong and fierce and honest and he realised she needed to know what she was getting into. She needed to know that the man she was marrying was never going to be the kind of husband she *should* have. It was only fair that she understood his limitations so he wouldn't let her down like this again because she'd know what to expect.

'I failed my mother. More than once. Really badly.'

Rosanna's eyes widened in her pale face and in the sunlight her gold hair glinted and suddenly he was tired of feeling frustrated. Somehow he felt compelled to confess everything to her—as if she really were the beautiful angel she resembled.

'You know Hugh never wanted me,' he muttered, needing her to understand just how desperate things had been. 'He tried to bully her into getting rid of me, but she wouldn't and once I was born he refused to acknowledge I was his son. She tried to manage on her own but she needed help. When she asked him for just a little support he threatened to call social services on her for neglect of me. He didn't want me, but if she didn't toe the line, he'd make sure *she* didn't get to keep me either.'

'What?' Rosanna looked shocked.

'Yeah,' he muttered. 'That much of a monster. He wanted us out of his life for good. He was the ultimate in selfish.'

'Your poor mother.'

She didn't know the half of it. 'He actually paid off other guys to say they'd been with her.' Leo watched the distress in Rosanna's eyes build but he couldn't stop himself telling her the truth of how awful it had been. 'He spread the rumour that she was easy and that I could be anyone's bastard. And of course he refused to do a DNA test his whole life.' Leo growled. 'My mother gave up. She didn't have the funds or the energy to fight him in court. Nor did I until much later. But the things he'd said caused a rift with her family. They believed him over her.'

'Leo, that's awful.'

They'd *both* been unwanted then and his outrage still burned. 'He made everyone believe she was a liar. But she worked so hard. It was the two of us against the world. She didn't resent me. I mean, she had every right to but she...' He trailed off, remembering how they'd had nothing but each other. 'She would've done anything for me and she did. I cost her everything she had. In the end, even her life.'

'How?' Rosanna asked softly with a shake of her head.

She didn't believe him. So pretty. So trusting in the best of him. He didn't want that burden any more. He didn't want to crush her when he fell from that pedestal.

'I worked part-time jobs from the age of nine after Hugh had rejected us again.' That was when he'd understood the reality of his mother's struggle. 'Anything to help her out. She always had two or three jobs on the go but even then we were broke all the time.' He sighed. 'In my teens when I was stronger I worked in a cool store. One night I decided to miss a shift at work. Just to have a night out with a couple of mates.'

He'd been working for years and had been tempted to a blowout. It hadn't seemed like a big deal at the time, just one night off after a hard week.

'But my boss phoned my mum, trying to track me down. There'd been an unusually large delivery that night and it needed sorting. Mum had only just finished her previous shift but my boss was angry and told her he'd fire me if I didn't come in.' He bowed his head. 'But I didn't answer my phone to either Mum or my boss. I was a stupid jerk. So Mum went in. She worked the shift for me. But she'd had a cough and working in that cool store for eight hours, being so run-down already, made it worse.' He couldn't look at Rosanna now. 'It only took a couple of days. The cough went to her lungs. She said she'd be fine. But she wasn't. Pneumonia.'

And he'd never missed a day of work since. Not until he'd taken Rosanna to Great Barrier Reef this week. And that had been work too, right? Of a different kind.

'It wasn't your fault.' Rosanna put a gentle hand on his shoulder.

'Of course it was,' he argued, stiffening beneath her touch. 'If I hadn't been selfish and lazy... She worked so hard for me and I let her down.' He hated himself for it. The feeling of helplessness had been absolute. Now the final humiliation spilled from him like poison. 'When it was evident how unwell she was, I went to Hugh Castle one last time.'

He'd wanted to transfer her to another hospital. Fight for second opinions. Anything that might've helped her. Even though he'd known it was too late by then. But he'd been desperate to try anything. 'I actually cried. I begged him for help.'

'And he wouldn't.'

Leo had failed. He'd been determined it would never happen again—he'd never allow himself to return to that utterly vulnerable, helpless position of losing someone he loved, of being unable to help them. It was easy enough when he kept people at a distance. Only now a wave of panic burned in his gut—because he had Rosanna and two children to be responsible for. His breathing quickened and he grasped at what had happened next—distracting himself by telling her the last.

'A year or so later Ash found me. He'd heard rumours and he was rebellious and bitter. He offered up some DNA to do a test. We'd see if we were related and that would be the proof I needed to prove Hugh's paternity.'

'He was angry with your father too?'

'Yeah. Maybe I'm lucky Hugh Castle didn't have the influence on my life the way he did with Ash.'

'But you took his name.'

'*Away* from him. Because it was the last thing he wanted to give me. So yes, I took it.'

He'd taken everything that old man had never wanted him to have. His name. His company. His whole life's work. 'And now I have his company. He knows—I told him my plans before he died. Ash invited me to see him and backed me fully. Fool that I am, I went. Thinking that perhaps on his damned deathbed he might finally be honest about who he was and what he'd done. That he might feel an inkling of remorse.'

'But he didn't.'

He'd taken pleasure in the man's impotent rage. He'd taken pleasure in making himself more successful than his cheating, denying father had ever been. The old man hadn't been able to do a thing to stop him.

'I've asked myself my whole life what was wrong with him. I've never figured out an answer that made any sense other than that he was just mean. That he liked to be in control and hold power over people. I won't be anything like him. Ever.'

Which meant he couldn't let Rosanna down or their babies down. But *family* wasn't something he'd ever wanted. It cost too much and he didn't know how to keep it safe or successful. He far preferred work, the challenge of making that a success—getting tangible results was something he could do well.

'My original surname was meaningless,' he muttered distractedly. 'Her family didn't support her, didn't believe her. So she left. She called me Leonardo after Da Vinci because she liked his sculptures. It's as good a reason as any. And I took Castle because it's a permanent reminder to everyone who wouldn't believe her that she was right. It's the only way I can honour her now.' He hated that she'd died before the truth had been proven. 'Because it's my fault she passed away when she did.'

'*No.*' Rosanna gazed into his eyes with such compassion he couldn't stand it.

'Her illness wasn't your fault,' she said. 'It was only one night—'

'When she was tired already,' he interrupted harshly. 'When she'd not been eating well because she'd been giving me most of what we had because I wouldn't stop growing. When she hadn't had enough sleep in years. When her asthma was aggravated by the damp house we lived in because we couldn't afford decent heating. That was all because of me. Because she had to make do with less to give *me* more.'

It was *entirely* because of him that it happened.

'And I bet you were the light of her life,' Rosanna said simply. 'She loved you. She wanted you. She fought to have you and keep you. And, yes, she did anything she could for you. That's what love is. It's awful what happened to her—but that lack of support was on her family, on your father. The other *adults* in her life. *Not* you.'

* * *

Rosanna watched the emotions flicker across Leo's face until he turned away from her. No wonder marriage and children weren't on his to-do list. The man had been so hurt—by a father who'd repeatedly refused to acknowledge him and then by the loss of his beloved mother, who'd sacrificed everything to have him. And he blamed himself fully for her death. There'd been no in-betweens. It had been so extreme for him.

'You should have been able to have some fun,' she said sadly. 'You were just a teenager.'

'Don't feel sorry for me, Rosanna.'

'Well, I do,' she said softly. 'I think all that just sucks. You were so alone and too young to deal with all of that. It wasn't fair.'

She regretted burning him for being a workaholic. Of course he was—he'd had to be just to survive. And then, because of the guilt he'd felt. It didn't matter what she or anyone said to him, she knew there'd always be a part within him that felt guilty about his mother's passing. Emotions weren't rational. No wonder he'd wanted to stay in control. No wonder he'd wanted to shield her from stress.

'I have a really good life,' he said quietly.

He had a really lonely life.

'She'd be pleased for me,' he added.

'She would. And proud.'

She turned him to face her and wound her arms around his waist. Relief flowed when he rested his head on hers and he accepted her simple embrace. But Rosanna knew pride in achievement wasn't everything. Pleasing someone, making them proud...that didn't really matter. What mattered was knowing that the person you loved was *happy*. That was what she wanted her parents to want for her, as she was sure Leo's mother would want for him. What she wanted for her babies. And, she realised, it was what she wanted for Leo. Honourable, hardworking, loyal, heartbroken Leo. She wanted *him* to be happy. She wanted to do everything she could to make his life better still.

And why was that?

Her heart soared and sank at the same time, tearing her in two with a wave of anxiety that she couldn't stem…

She loved him.

CHAPTER FOURTEEN

THEY DIDN'T LAUGH on the flight back to Sydney. Rosanna didn't spill any salty snacks, didn't eat any—she wasn't hungry. He sat near to her but there was the slightest withdrawal. More than mere silence. Maybe he was thinking about work already and all the things he had to catch up on since being away. But she was anxious it wasn't that. She was anxious about *everything*.

Dinner last night had been an art of distraction. In bed after there'd been his touch again—a silent, desperate touch. She'd clung, unable to hold back her need to embrace him. She couldn't tell him she loved him, self preservation warned her. He'd been quiet since. So had she. Maybe she was being over-sensitive—feeling vulnerable about her own emotions—but she couldn't help feeling he regretted all that he'd said.

Back at the Sydney penthouse she discovered Leo hadn't wasted any time. She found her belongings had been dried out and sent over. Her cuttings had been brought to the terrace garden, even Axel the axolotl had made the move.

'Is everything going to survive?' he asked.

'I think so.' She smiled at him. 'Thank you. This was a massive effort.'

'Not my effort really. I just got staff onto it.' He watched her ruefully. 'I'm sorry I didn't tell you about it right away.'

'It's okay, I understand why you waited.'

He feared her vulnerability. He glanced away. She felt wariness at this new intimacy. On holiday it had been easy, now there were other issues to navigate.

'We should dine with your parents tonight,' he said suddenly. 'Have you got something to wear?'

The prospect terrified her but she knew she had to face them. 'I can find something. And yes, I know I can buy something if I want to.'

She waved the bank card that had also been waiting for her at the penthouse. He'd insisted on organising money for her. She'd accepted, now understanding why he needed to do that too. His need to ensure her well-being was part of the deal. But he'd learn that *she* needed independence too. And respect. They could work on that. She knew he was trying—he'd just apologised, after all.

After Leo left to go to his office, Rosanna phoned her boss to let him know to expect her resignation. She offered online support to her students until her replacement was hired. Given her flat was currently uninhabitable, he understood. She emailed her students to let them know and got some immediate replies that made her smile. She'd figure out a job in the future, but for now she needed to work things out properly with Leo. They needed more time to build on the foundations they'd begun to form on their trip away. She went shopping, unable to resist the desire to impress not her mother, but Leo.

He returned from work surprisingly early. She smoothed down the sides of her dress. It was floral silk, sensual to the touch. Slim fitting, but she didn't mind if her slightly wonky waist and lean to the left were obvious.

'Is this okay?'

He hardly glanced at her. 'Gorgeous. Let's go.'

Her nerves built even more. He was definitely distant and her heart shrank.

'I spoke to my mother earlier,' she said as Leo drove them out of the basement garage.

'How was she?'

'She sounded excited on the phone but didn't press for more information, which is unusual.'

Leo narrowed his eyes on the red traffic light ahead. 'I offered them a deal at a new property we've picked up in Queensland.'

'Pardon?' Rosanna swivelled to stare at him.

'A contract on a resort we're redoing there. It's a new acquisition. Something different. It's not a large project, but we'll see how they go.'

She was stunned. 'So the proposal bargain you made the other day—'

'Was a mistake,' he interrupted her smoothly. 'As you rightly recognised at the time. This isn't a reward for saying yes.'

But that was exactly what it was. And it felt wrong. 'How can it be anything else? You can't give them the contract. Cronyism and nepotism aren't your thing.'

She'd respected him for that.

'They can't be homeless, Rosanna. I can't allow that to happen.'

So he was paying them off?

Her parents were now getting everything they'd wanted—business contracts and a society wedding. Their only child marrying a powerful, wealthy man— creating a permanent relationship they'd always benefit from. But she didn't want them winning all that—they'd have learned nothing from their own mistakes. And she certainly didn't want him feeling obligated to look after *all* her family. It made her not just a responsibility to him, but a burden.

And suddenly she was furious. 'Have you negotiated with them already?'

'I haven't told them about the babies. I thought we could do that together.'

Her jaw dropped. 'You thought?' Her fury flared. 'You've done *all* the thinking on this.'

Just what she *didn't* want.

'I didn't want the contract mess and their problems getting in the way of our wedding,' he said.

He'd gone behind her back. *Again.*

'I thought we'd talked about making these decisions together.'

'This was a business decision. Not a personal one.'

'Rubbish, it's to do with my *parents*,' she snapped. 'You thought you could decide the "best" way to solve this without even discussing it with me?'

She was a pawn, not a person. She had no real voice. She was not a priority. Again.

'That's not how it was.' His frustration sounded. 'I've had a business relationship with your parents for longer than I've known you.'

'But this *is* personal. This is because of me and what's happened between *us*. Otherwise you'd have just cancelled their contract and never looked back. It's everything *you* didn't want, Leo.'

'Things have changed.'

What mattered to him most was the impact on his business. That was what mattered to her parents most too. *She* was not the priority here. And she never would be. Nor would her children. He might think he'd done it for her. But he hadn't.

'I didn't want to upset you,' he said.

'Why would it matter if I got upset? People get upset all the time. Then they get over it. We could have worked it out.'

His jaw tightened. 'I was hoping to save you stress.'

'You've just caused me more.' She was so hurt. 'You're used to doing anything and everything you want, calling all the shots, but that's not how this can work with us. I thought you understood that. Why couldn't you trust me to talk to me?'

They'd got nowhere. She'd been fooling herself for thinking they'd connected not just on a physical level but an emotional one. That he'd opened up to her. That he understood her needs as well as her understanding his. But he'd gone all high-handed boss again. Solving everyone's problems for them as if he were responsible for everyone and everything. He did it without consultation. Without trust. And without that, there could be no future—not the kind she wanted.

In the light of her *own* emotions, her own vulnerability to him, she knew she couldn't do this. She couldn't accept this for her future.

'I thought you didn't want them to end up homeless,' he growled.

Of course she didn't. That wasn't the point right now. 'Why wouldn't you talk to me about it when you knew I'd want you to?'

He glared at her. 'Because I knew you'd say no.'

'So you just did what you wanted anyway? Despite already knowing it's not what I would want.' She was so hurt. 'Because you feel responsibility for me.'

'Naturally I do.' He looked furious. 'I got you *pregnant*.'

It came back to that. Of course it did. And it would *always* come back to that. If fate hadn't intervened, they never would have come to this—to her living with him, agreeing to marry him.

It wasn't because he'd fallen in love with her.

He'd paid a high price for that night. He'd even tried to do the right thing then. He'd used contraception. He'd been courteous. He'd done everything right. When really all he'd wanted was a few moments of escape for himself. She related to that. She really, really did. But now he was stuck with her. And he was a man who took his responsibilities so very seriously.

He should be free and laughing as he had when they were out on the reef. Carefree and having fun. He should be out dating, playing the field. Finding his perfect match. Getting over the heartbreak of his mother's passing. Learning it was okay not to work all the time. Learning that loving again would be worth it.

Not *settling* for her because he felt he had to. Because he couldn't *not* do the right thing. She didn't want to be that person to him. The one he 'had' to be with, who he 'had' to look after. Fate was cruel. The burden of her and their twins was the last thing he deserved or needed.

The worst thing was, she wanted so much more from him. And that was unfair of her, wasn't it? She'd fallen for him knowing she was never going to be the right wife for him. She wasn't who he'd fall in love with. How could he? So now he was working so hard to make the best of it. To make her believe they could make it work. But she wasn't who he really wanted. This was only because of circumstance. He only wanted to marry her because he had to. And it hurt. It really, really hurt. Because now that whole trip felt like a lie.

'This isn't relevant, Rosanna.' He tried to dismiss it.

'It's totally relevant. It's everything.'

'We don't have time to talk about this—'

'We don't have the time not to. This matters.'

'It doesn't. It's fixed.'

'*Nothing* is fixed.' She shook her head at him—at the way he wanted to shut this down. 'You're afraid of emotional conflict.'

He flinched. 'No, I'm not.'

'You don't want anyone to get too close.'

'How can you say that? I told you things I've never told anyone.'

'And you regret it.'

'Right now? Yes. Because you're using what you know of my past to misinterpret my actions now.'

'No, I'm seeing your actions for what they are. You're a straight-up guy just trying to do the right thing. And you'll always try to do the right thing by anyone.'

He stared at her. 'And the problem is…?'

'You don't want people equating you with your father.'

His jaw clenched. 'Of course I don't.'

'That's the real reason you want us to marry, right? Because you don't want to be seen as being like him. Not being there for your children. Not recognising them.'

He didn't deny it.

It was the *only* reason that really mattered to him. He was desperately proving that he wasn't like the man who'd seeded him. He'd do that over and over. This *was* about his past. Not about her at all. Or even what was truly best for their children.

It was still about reputation. Her life would be bound for ever by 'what's best for the business' dictates. Just as her whole childhood had been. She'd never been the priority—not number one in her parents' lives. Not in Leo's either—her future partner's. And that was not what she wanted for her children. To come second to the business. To reputation. To what others thought. The measure of success. To make all decisions upon that.

She'd allowed it to happen. She'd tried to be what her parents wanted. But now she had her own children to think about and she didn't want them trying to live up to—or break away from—parental reputation or expectation. She wanted them to be free. And in order for that to happen, *she* needed to be free. And to do that— she had to be *honest*. And brave.

'There are a lot of factors contributing to the decision for us to marry, Rosanna.'

'But not the usual one.' The most important one for her. The emotional one that he clearly didn't feel.

'You mean…' He trailed off.

'You can't even say it?' She laughed a little brokenly. 'Love. Leo, yes. I'm talking about love.'

'We've both known from the beginning this has nothing to do with love.'

It had *everything* to do with it.

'You think you don't deserve it,' she said. 'Not just because of your mother. Not just because you don't want to mess up a marriage the way your father did. You don't want to mess *anything* up so you don't engage at all.'

'Look who's talking.' He snorted. 'You're the one who hides in a lab all day, still trying to be something for someone else. Who could only have some fun when she pretended to be someone else.'

'It wasn't that I pretended to be someone else,' she argued. 'You were right. That night with you I was able to be myself—with no preconceived ideas, no expectations.' He'd encouraged her to be herself. Accepted her as she was. He'd told her she was strong and she'd believed him. 'I could just be me. And you wanted me then.'

But he didn't love her.

'And I want you now. We want *each other*,' he said grimly. 'So why are we arguing? Why isn't that enough?'

Because it wouldn't last for him. And she didn't want to wake up every morning and wonder if that was the day when he decided he didn't want her any more. 'Because one day one of us might want someone else.'

He stared at her. 'Might that not happen anyway?' he asked cruelly. 'Whether we state we're in love or not?'

His cynicism broke her heart. 'You don't believe in it.'

'No, I don't. There's a decent arrangement, Rosanna. And that is absolutely what we can have. There's loyalty and honouring the contract we'll make. *That's* what marriage is. A contract.'

Purely business.

'So there's no consideration in your life for loving someone? There's responsibility. There's protectiveness. There's passion. What's the missing piece of the puzzle?' She stared at him. 'Why can't you call it what it is?'

'Because it isn't what you want it to be,' he growled. 'It never will be.'

He didn't feel for her that way.

'What if it is for me?' she said. 'What if I said I'd fallen in love with you? And I want you to love me. *That's* what I want.'

'Rosanna…'

'Couldn't we have it all?' She gazed at him sadly. 'Why can't I?'

His face froze. 'I'm sorry. I can give you everything else. Everything—'

'*But* the one thing I really want. The one thing that's *free*.'

'It isn't though.' He scowled. 'I don't have the resources for that in my account. I don't have the means or the capacity to give you what you want.'

'That's not true,' she whispered.

'Not for *anyone*,' he continued harshly. 'I don't have it, Rosanna. Never did. Never will.'

She glared at him. The way he'd retreated behind his wall of seriousness. 'You think you're strong? Focused? It's not discipline, it's *denial*. And it's based in fear.'

'I know what it feels like to have nothing and to lose everything.'

'I know. And I'm sorry, but that doesn't mean you never strive again.'

'I spend my *life* striving.'

'For *one* element,' she yelled. 'The *least* important. Work doesn't matter. It doesn't keep you warm at night.' She was furious with him. 'You didn't want to be like him.'

'It's about responsibility—'

'That's just control in disguise. You want to control what you give and to whom you give it. Every bit as much as he did.'

'I'm *nothing* like him,' he roared, stopping the car at a red light.

'Are you sure?' she asked bitterly. 'Because it seems to me that he was incapable of giving love. And also of receiving it. And isn't that you?'

His withdrawal was absolute. The rigidity of his expression. The cold anger in his eyes.

'You don't want that from me,' she said. 'You don't want my love.'

'You only offer it because you're confusing lust for love. Because you're tired and emotional.'

'Are you serious? Are you going to say this is hormones talking?'

'Isn't it?'

'Don't tell me I'm tired. I'm fine. I'm strong and capable and I'll survive. More than survive. But I *am* tired of not having my voice heard. Of not being someone's number one. Of not being more important than anything else to someone.'

He froze again. 'Then if what I'm offering isn't enough, don't feel you have to stay.'

Her heart tore as she swung on the door handle and stumbled out of the car, clutching her little handbag close. She frantically waved at a taxi going past.

'Rosanna!'

She ignored him. He'd just told her to go. It was the most honest thing he'd said all afternoon.

CHAPTER FIFTEEN

Leo Castle refused to be angry. Rosanna walking out was the best thing. Definitely best for her. And it had been good to remind himself of his painful past because now he remembered what he wanted to be, how he wanted to live—with honour and utter independence. Security and safety for Rosanna and the babies was paramount and his way to help them achieve that was with his work. Always with work.

Finally his cool-headed business brain switched on.

She'd been right in the beginning. There was no need for them to marry. He'd get them an apartment, set the children up with trust funds, ensure Rosanna had more financial support than she could ever need. It was straightforward really. Why had he got so tied up in knots about securing so-called legitimacy and security for them? For thinking that they needed to be *married*? For thinking that *he* was integral to making that happen? Quite the reverse was true. They'd be better off *without* him being overly influential in their lives.

But here he was once again wide awake in the small hours of the night, overthinking his most personal problems. The things he regretted. The moments he wanted to redo but couldn't.

She deserved more. She ought to have felt that spark with someone more worthy than him. Of course he'd failed her. He didn't know what he was doing and didn't think he could ever learn. Because there it was, the fear that, with a father like Hugh Castle, he was missing some elemental aspect of humanity. He could work hard. He could think well. But loving someone the way they needed to be loved? Listening to them? Meeting their needs? No. He'd failed at that. Again.

In his office, hours later, Leo looked down at the list of text messages. Rosanna had sent the same message every day for a week already.

I'm fine. Will be in touch again soon.

She was letting him know she was fine. Not where she was. Not what she was doing. Not who she was with. Just very courteous and polite so he wouldn't worry.

He wanted to throw his new phone into the goddamn ocean. These messages were rubbish. Not enough. Not ever enough.

But he refused to phone her. Refused to track where she might be. Refused to write more than his monosyllabic reply. She'd wanted space. He had to give it to her. And he reminded himself, yet again, that he'd done the right thing. The *only* thing to have done. For *her.* He couldn't give her all that she wanted so he'd let her go. That was right, wasn't it?

Only he hadn't *let* her go, he'd *told* her to leave. And he hated remembering the look in her eyes at that moment.

She would be better off with someone else eventually. Leo felt capable of violence at the thought of some other man in her life, but he clamped down on every muscle. He didn't want her to be unhappy and she would be eventually, if she were forced to stay with him, living a life in which he couldn't give her everything she needed. He couldn't do the emotional stuff. He didn't know how to.

He should have been feeling better by now. It was over a week already. But he wasn't. And, damn it, he *was* angry. He was freaking furious.

Why had she pushed? *Why* had she asked for more? *Why* didn't she understand he'd offered all he had to give? *Why* couldn't that be enough for her?

But why should she settle for less?

Rosanna Gold deserved the best of everything and everyone.

Only there was that selfish bit in him that still wanted to keep her for himself. That greedy part of him that tormented him every damn minute with memories—teasing him with sensations and sounds. He remembered her lilting quiet comments, that chime of laughter that became so infectious when she let it go, the softness of her pale skin, her slender waist and that one spot on her back where he could feel where steel met spine.

She was strong, the thief in his garden. And she was sweet.

He couldn't believe that she really was in love with him. He'd told her it was lust clouding everything— as it had clouded his world for weeks. Thanks to him, she'd fallen pregnant. With *twins*. She'd fallen out even worse with her parents. She'd had to quit her job. He'd completely messed up her life.

No way could she love him given all that.

* * *

Rosanna showered and dressed, glad it was time to get moving. She'd been awake for an hour already and had dwelled long enough for today. She liked to walk to the plant nursery the long way—via the beachfront. She'd found room in a flat share—agreed to a month by month lease, which gave her flexibility for now. And while she'd started at the nursery just on customer service, her boss had quickly realised her knowledge base and had upped her responsibility with the actual plants. So life was going okay, right? Only on the inside, she wasn't quite okay. Not *yet*.

She missed him.

They'd laughed together. They'd discovered they had stuff in common. She'd enjoyed their conversations—she'd found him fascinating and funny. He'd electrified her life. She'd thought they'd entered their own little world on the reef—one that they'd bring back with them. She'd thought that he trusted her...

She'd been an idiot. Leo Castle didn't truly trust anyone and he never would. He'd temporarily allowed her his body, offered her financial and physical stability, even a kind of companionship. As *friends*. But that was where it ended for him. Whereas for her it had been impossible not to make a far deeper emotional investment. She'd not meant for it to happen. But it had. She'd fallen in love with him. So easily. So quickly. So stupidly.

As she neared the nursery she turned her phone on and tapped the screen.

I'm fine. Will be in touch again soon.

She sent the text to him at the same time each day. Then she sent the same to her parents. Then she turned off her phone again—mostly to stop herself hoping she'd get a decent response. Her parents hadn't questioned her as to why she'd suddenly decided to move or why she'd not explained her relationship with Leo. Maybe they were too busy with their new contract for him in Queensland already. And Leo had barely replied at all. The first time he'd answered.

Let me know where you are so we can make arrangements for the future.

She hadn't done that yet. She'd just sent the same message. Since then he'd just replied OK.

She knew hiding was cowardly but right now it was all she could manage. Working was good. Working was a distraction from the brutal fact that she'd asked him to love her and he'd told her to leave. That she'd ruined what they might have had. She'd not been enough—a disappointment yet again. She'd let their children down.

Leo didn't want her with him because she couldn't accept what he could offer. But no more would she accept *less* than she needed. No more would she try to be what someone *else* wanted. Not for the rest of her life.

She'd never been someone's number one. Maybe she never would be. But she'd put herself first and by extension her children too. Because *she* needed to be a better example to them than she'd been until now. She needed to demonstrate self-worth to them so they would grow up strong and happy and capable of loving and being loved.

So at least now she was holding her own in life. New town. New flat. New job. New friends even—her work-mates were friendly, her flatmates too. She'd made more friends here already than she'd made at the university in all those years.

But that night as she walked home via the beach path, she turned her phone back on and saw she had a message. Her heart stilled. It was her parents. There was some waffle, nervousness even, but also a note of concern she'd not heard before. And then…

We miss you. Is there anything we can do for you? Anything you need?

Her mum's questions ever so slightly soothed a deep wound. For the first time they'd finally asked what—if anything—they could do for her. They'd asked to know her thoughts and how she felt. And she'd tell them. Soon.

She'd not meant to scare them, which was why she'd messaged each day. But she needed to do this now for *herself*. So she'd build the courage to eventually figure out some kind of working relationship with Leo.

It stung that he'd made no effort to contact her more directly, or to find her. Which meant he was truly okay with her leaving. Regardless of the reputation he cared about so damned much, he hadn't wanted her to stay. And that hurt.

A stupid part of her had hoped he'd turn up, but over the course of the last fortnight that hope was starting to fade. She'd come to realise that right from the start their entanglement had meant something different to her than it had to him. And if he wasn't ready to open up to someone, to her? That had to be okay. She couldn't force him to. It was okay for him not to have fallen in love with her.

Yet while she knew that rationally, emotionally she was *devastated*. She'd opened up to him. She'd given herself to him—she'd wanted to give him everything. But he didn't want it. He didn't want her.

He'd be in her life for ever. He was the father of her children. So she knew she had to work out a way where she could cope with seeing him…and, eventually, seeing him with someone else.

She needed time to build the strength to face that. Time and energy and courage. And she wasn't going to apologise for taking it now.

Leo didn't want to work any more, but he had to. It was the only thing he knew—the only way to hold back the emotions festering inside him. He couldn't face going back to his penthouse—it was filled with her plants— but he'd had to do that too. He was terrified of killing her freaking fish.

For some unfathomable reason he couldn't outsource the responsibility of Axel. He now knew more about the care and feeding of axolotls than he'd ever imagined possible. He'd been working round the clock, even when he was at home keeping Axel company—avoiding any downtime in which he might start thinking about her.

Who was he kidding? He thought about her *all the time*.

Losing someone was the worst feeling in the world. He'd never wanted to go through that devastation again.

He'd never let anyone close enough. But he was devastated right now.

So he went to the office. It was the only thing he could think to do, even though he'd never been more sick of it in his life. Hours later he glanced up at the knock on his door and watched his manager, Petra, come in with a wary look on her face. When he'd first got back to the office he'd learned she'd gone to Melbourne to sign up a new client. Now she'd returned and looked as if she were entering a scorpion's nest as she presented the proposal she'd gone away to deliver.

'You don't mind that I went ahead and did this without consulting you?' she asked as he skimmed the fine print.

Rosanna's words came back to him. She'd said she felt sorry for his staff because he was such a micromanager. He'd scoffed. But maybe she'd been right?

'Of course not,' he muttered. 'I was away. I trust your judgement.' Then he paused and looked up at Petra. 'You enjoyed it?'

'Yeah, once I got past the performance anxiety.'

He felt that twist of guilt tighten. 'You did a good job,' he said.

'So it's okay with you?'

Petra's double-checking for reassurance made him feel even worse. Maybe he was more iron fist and less 'velvet glove' than he'd realised.

'It's more than okay.' A rush of thinking derailed him. Allowing his team greater responsibility would free up some of his own time. 'Actually I'd like you to take a look at the project list and rank a few you'd like to take greater control of. I need to delegate more and I'd like you to be first in line.'

Petra's jaw dropped. 'Seriously?'

'You'll need a couple of assistants too,' he added, thinking it through and feeling the certainty of the direction in his bones. 'Otherwise you'll end up like me.'

Frozen on the inside. Incapable of giving someone the time and emotional support they needed. Wedded to work. Unable to trust anyone. He'd always needed to see it all, know it all, decide it all, himself—to have that total control.

Suddenly he didn't care about work any more. It had lost its stranglehold on him. And he didn't want to be controlling everything for everyone all the time. He wanted a damned break.

He'd been using work as an excuse to avoid intimacy. Using it as a vehicle to prove himself over and over again—but to whom and for what? *What* was he fighting so bloody hard for any more?

Far too late he realised he'd been fighting in the wrong field of his life.

He'd let his mother down, and the impossibility of making it up to her, the impossibility of fighting for his rights—and hers—from his father...bogged him down. He'd failed in all of that.

I bet you were the light of her life.

Rosanna's words haunted him, seduced him, made him feel better. Rationally he'd always known she was right—that he'd been young, that his mother might've got sick anyway, that the far greater responsibility fell on the shoulders of his father.

But *believing* it was harder. Rosanna had said he

was like his father too. That he was too controlling. Too afraid of relinquishing control.

Control. Discipline. Denial.

All facets of the same stone that his heart had become. The stone weighed too heavy now and the resulting hurt was unbearable. Because Rosanna Gold was lovely. Kind. Funny. Dutiful, even when she didn't want to be. Loyal to a fault. Even to people who'd let her down. She still tried. Indefatigably trying to do her best for others. For her students. For her damned plants and funny fish. For anyone and anything she allowed in her life. Which actually *wasn't* that many people or things. Because *she'd* been hurt before too.

But she'd wanted to love him. She'd tried to love him. And he hadn't let her.

He'd turned away from the light that she'd brought him. The light that she was. And now he was in darkness. Now he realised that he wanted that light—that *love*—more than anything. Even though he was terrified of losing it—of her taking it away, or not wanting him any more.

So he'd not believed her. And he'd not listened to her. He'd ignored his own damn actions—and said no to her. The overprotectiveness he'd felt hadn't been about the babies. It was about *her*.

He'd done to her what his father had done to him. The thing he'd said he'd never do. He'd denied her truth—the existence of her feelings. And he'd denied his *own*. He'd not allowed himself to have faith in the thing he wanted most. And he'd hurt her as well as himself. It was the worst thing he could have done to her—when he knew that she ached inside to be seen and heard, to be valued by that one special person who paid attention and noticed the little things. To care for her the way she'd care in return. Openly, unconditionally. For always.

He'd been so *arrogant* to think that his way was the only way. But there was only one thing he was certain of now. He didn't just want Rosanna back in his life. He *needed* her. And he loved her. He just had to convince her of all of that… Because what if he'd hurt her too much to be forgiven?

CHAPTER SIXTEEN

'ARE YOU SURE there's nothing else I can do?' Rosanna called to her boss as she finished watering the seedlings.

'No, you head home. Thank you!'

On her way back through the shop she couldn't resist pausing to tweak the terrarium display. She loved that the shop sold not just plants but terrariums and aquariums as well. They were all so pretty and working amongst them inspired her.

She glanced up as someone stalked towards her—she smiled, expecting it to be a customer. But it wasn't a customer. It was a man she knew.

No. Her heart stopped.

She spoke before he had the chance to. 'I'm at work. I can't talk now.'

'Your shift finished ten minutes ago.'

How did he know that? *Control freak.*

'How did you find me?' she asked, her emotional control slipping already. 'An investigator?'

'You didn't give me much choice.' The faintest smile curved his mouth.

She hardened her heart against it. But she couldn't stop herself drinking in the sight of him. Leo Castle wasn't in a suit. He wore loose trousers and a grey tee and looked as if he hadn't eaten or slept in a month. Deep shadows beneath his eyes highlighted the burning over-brightness of his indigo irises. His voice was as creaky as his appearance—as if it hadn't been properly cared for in days.

He stared down at her, seeming to try to see right through her. 'Rosanna.'

Her heart pounded at the emotive whisper. She willed herself to look away from him and not be bewitched all over again, struggling to find the strength. He was *here*.

She didn't want to see him. She'd been doing *well*. She wasn't ready and this wasn't *fair*.

'I told you I needed more time—'

'I'll leave if that's what you want.' His voice was so husky. 'But I hoped you might hear me out. Just briefly.'

The problem was she couldn't cope with her own emotions—the initial elation at seeing him again followed by the instant torpedoing of that excitement because she'd remembered, *he didn't want her*.

Why, then, was he here?

'It's Thursday afternoon,' she said. 'You should be at work.'

'I've switched to a four-day week. Thursday is my new day off.'

She stared at him nonplussed—because he looked so damn serious about that.

'It's true. I'm trying to change a few things. I need to.'

'What's that?' She nodded at the strip of green leaf he was holding.

He glanced down and a rueful grin broke the seriousness. 'I noticed it when I was walking along the beach earlier waiting for you to be finished here.' He held it up so she could see it properly. 'I thought you could try growing another cutting.' He regarded the limp thing sadly. 'I would have ripped out the whole plant but remembered you like growing something from not very much. I think that's a challenge you enjoy.' He gazed directly into her eyes. 'And I think you don't want to destroy something in order to create something new.'

'Sometimes you can't get something to grow no matter how much you want to.'

'That doesn't mean you stop trying,' he replied.

Leo couldn't stop staring at her. She looked gorgeous. In loose trousers and a white tee that was knotted at her waist that still didn't show any sign of the twin secrets growing inside. Her glorious hair was swept up in a messy bun and secured with a white scarf. He'd watched her smiling at customers, insanely jealous of the two minutes of her time that they got. She'd looked happy and healthy and stupidly that had made him angrier. Made him more afraid. That smile had fallen from her face the second she saw him. So now he was terrified.

'Can we go somewhere to talk?' he asked gruffly.

There was a moment where he thought she might refuse. But then she turned.

'You can walk me back to my flat,' she said.

The one he'd learned she shared with three other people. He was jealous of them too.

He'd been awake all night plotting what to say, how to say it, where to say it, but now he was here, he'd forgotten all his great plans and didn't know where to begin. Now he was with her, all he wanted to do was pull her close and kiss her. Exactly what he wasn't supposed to do. Instead he put one foot in front of the other and walked out with her.

'Did you need to see for yourself that I'm okay?' She sounded bitter—as if she thought he'd not believed her messages. 'Because I am.'

'I know and I'm glad,' he said huskily. His heart was beating too fast. He paused on the beach; he couldn't go a step further. He drew in a breath. 'I've asked my managers to take on some of my workload. I'm serious about Thursdays—or whatever day might be best. I'm trying to let go of my micromanagement issue.'

She blinked. 'Good for you.'

'So that's given me more time to think.' He paused because his brain just wouldn't work properly now—every thought had scattered upon seeing her again. 'I've been feeding Axel. I thought if I could keep him alive there might be hope for me...' None of this was coming out right. 'I wish we could go back to the reef.'

Wariness, sadness, bloomed in her eyes. 'You only took me there to convince me to do what you wanted. You just wanted me to say yes to marrying you.'

'I would have done anything to get you to say yes to me.' He admitted it freely. 'But I never stopped to ask myself *why* I really wanted that so much.' He couldn't resist reaching out to take her hand. 'I also swallowed my pride and offered your parents something I said I never would. Why did I do that?'

'Because you thought you had to, to make everything okay. To win. To stave off any future conflict.'

'Again. That's partly true. But *why* did it matter so

much?' He needed her to understand. 'I've been in conflict my whole life, Rosanna—'

'I know,' she interrupted softly. 'Fighting the whole time. You must be so sick of it.'

'I thrive on contractual challenges. On problem-solving. But with you there's always been a different edge.'

She fell silent.

'I watched you that night. You were so beautiful, so curious. You appreciated something so small with such intensity. And made me curious and then you suddenly opened up like some gorgeous flower.'

She pulled her hand free of his, her shoulders hunching inwards. 'It should only have been that one night.'

'No. You're wrong. I was wrong for letting you leave then. And for letting you leave the other day.'

Rosanna's blood beat like drums, deafening her when she needed to hear most acutely. 'Why are you here? I offered you everything I had and you didn't want it.' He'd hurt her. 'But I'm fine now. I don't want your excuses. We can just move on.' She blinked back tears.

'I can't move on.'

'Why?'

He took hold of her shoulders and bent his knees so he could see into her eyes. 'Because you matter to me. Because you're everything to me.'

She dragged in a scalding breath. 'No...'

'That night I really liked you, Rosanna,' he said quietly, urgently, his words tumbling. 'Yeah, I took one look and wanted, but when you started talking I wanted to listen. I wanted to be around you. And the more time I had with you, the more I wanted and that freaked me out.' He released a harsh breath. 'I'm not good at building relationships… I don't have much practice and it scares the hell out of me. And for the first time I wanted to do things *other* than work and that was scary too. Because that's not controllable in the same way. I'm sorry it has taken me so long to realise what should have been so obvious. I did all that on the reef, with your flat, with your parents… Not because I felt I should, but because I've fallen in love with you. Only I resisted admitting that the day you left because it terrified me. You could hurt me like no one else. You *did*. I never wanted someone to ever get that close.'

She curled her hands into fists. 'I never wanted to hurt you. *You* did that when you pushed me away.'

'I know,' he said simply. 'And I am so sorry I hurt you.'

Suddenly she was shaking and he swept his arms around her.

'I'm sorry, I'm sorry, I'm sorry.' He whispered it against her hair. 'Because that's what happened.' His breath caught. 'I hurt you before you could hurt me.'

'You sent me away.' It still hurt.

'I was an idiot. I was afraid and that made me angry. I thought you were about to leave anyway…sending you away was me getting in first. Because I couldn't stand the thought of your rejection. I couldn't cope. And I'm so sorry.'

He held her closer, cradling her as the tears finally fell.

'You're number one to *me*, Rosanna. You're *everything* to me. And without you…' His voice broke. 'I don't want that world any more. You were right. I tried to control everything because I was afraid. Losing someone hurts, Rosanna.' He struggled for composure. 'And I'm lost without you.'

She gripped his T-shirt, unable to answer. Her throat was too tight. Her tears too heavy.

'I don't want anything but *you*. You with your fiery hair and freckles and skin that's so soft and so revealing. You with your quiet way of seeing the world. Your eye for detail. You're *my* idea of perfect. Just as you are. I want to steal you away to remote beaches so we can enjoy the sunsets. I want to dance with you—and I've never wanted to dance with anyone before. I want to stop and savour the small moments with you. See the things you see.'

'Leo.'

'I didn't mean to ignore your wishes or belittle your input or make you feel like you weren't my priority. I just wanted to protect you. But I screwed up.'

'And I overreacted,' she whispered, tears tracking down her face. 'I felt insecure and I flipped. I worried you were only doing all this because you felt you had to.'

'I do have to.' He smiled at her. 'Because I love you. But I'm terrified I am going to let you down. I'm terrified I'm going to let the babies down. I don't know how to be a dad.'

'Leo…'

'I couldn't look after my mother. I couldn't help her when she needed it most.'

'You're the most caring, most responsible man I know. You cared for me when I fell asleep on you that first night on the island. I saw you sneaking snacks to that little lizard. You tried to fix my flooded flat and ensured my plants didn't die... I don't know how to look after these babies either and learning might take us some time, but the *desire* to care...that's innate. And you have it no less than anyone else. In fact you have it *more* than most. The only problem is that sometimes you do it without consultation.' She smiled at him with regret. 'I shouldn't have said you were like your father. You're nothing like him.'

'You were right about my need for control.' He closed his eyes. 'There was a lot in my life I couldn't control for a really long time. So then I focused on what I *could* to the exclusion of almost everything else. And now I'm rusty at releasing my grip.'

She sighed. 'I don't want you to ever let me go,' she whispered.

'It might be hard for me not to be overprotective. It's going to take some practice at talking these things through with you and not just going ahead and trying to fix them on my own. But I really want to try.'

She loved that he wanted to try for her.

'I don't want you thinking I'm here because of duty or responsibility. This isn't actually about the babies. I'm here for *you*.'

A moan of raw emotion escaped and he swept her close and kissed her. He was here, offering everything she wanted, and she so badly wanted to believe in him. But she needed more of everything from him.

'Every time I take a breath it hurts because I know you're not beside me,' he said. 'You're not wandering off the path to look at some random tiny thing. You're not showing me so very much in all those little things.

You're not there when I get home. So home is hollow in a way it never has been before. Please come back with me.'

'Do you mean it?' Elation slowly filled her cold, cavernous heart—until his love filled it to overflowing.

But she shivered at the thought of what might have been. 'We might never have found each other again if I hadn't come to Ash's office that day.'

'So let's be grateful that we did and not lose each other again. Ever.' He released her hair from its clasp, running his hand through the waves. 'Maybe our paths would've crossed eventually. You were coming back to Sydney. I would've seen you.'

She chuckled. 'You think fate would've intervened?'

'I have no idea. I am just eternally grateful to your parents for bringing you back into my life that day—the best thing they've done aside from having you in the first place.'

She glanced up at him, nibbling on her lip. 'What are we going to do about them?'

He smiled down at her. 'We'll manage them *together*, okay?'

'Okay.' She drew a steadying breath. 'Will you come to my little flat with me now?' she asked. 'Please?'

His face lit up—double dimples, wide smile, love in his eyes. 'Thought you'd never ask.'

She walked faster than she'd walked in years, super-glad her flatmates would all still be at work. She *needed* him.

As soon as they were inside her door she turned to him and he didn't hold back. He picked her up, bracing her against the wall as he kissed her so hard she now understood how desperately he'd suffered through the long hours of loneliness and misery too. They'd endured an awful separation. They never would again.

'Please,' he growled, shaking with the effort to go both slow and fast, gentle and passionate. 'I missed you,' he muttered, pressing kisses against her hair with every other word. 'It scares me how much I missed you.'

She heard the break in his voice and lifted her gaze to see him. The vulnerability in his eyes devastated her.

'I know,' she breathed, her tears spilling again. 'It's been awful.'

He hoisted her up. 'Not any more.'

'No. Because you're here.'

He filled her with his strength and vitality and all that gorgeous, glorious intensity. It was better than anything—more sublime, more intense. The power of him was fully focused on her and nothing, nothing at all, was held back. Out of control completely, she shook in his arms—from pleasure this time, not heartbreak. And he matched her. His arms were like steel bands and it was the sweetest, sharpest sensation in the world.

'Love me,' she breathed almost deliriously. 'Love me the way I love you.'

'I do. That and more, darling. You have *everything* of me.'

He held her so close, making her believe with every kiss, every touch, every vow. Again and again he promised and assured until her belief in his word was imprinted on every cell in her body.

'I'm here,' he growled. 'With you. For you. And I'll love you as hard and as best I can until I'm no more.'

'Yes.'

He was her for ever.

EPILOGUE

A little over two years later

'ARE YOU READY?' Leo Castle strode out to the terrace and saw his wife ensconced at the table, bent over a large piece of paper with a container of sharp coloured pencils beside her.

His heart soared at the sight; he loved it when she was deep in concentration like this.

'I just need five more minutes,' she murmured, not looking up from her drawing. 'This bit is almost there.'

He sighed theatrically and shook his head mournfully. 'And you once told me I was a workaholic...'

At that she glanced up and sent him a laughing look. 'And you're not still?'

'Absolutely not,' he declared with a wink. He tried hard but admittedly there were times when their Thursday afternoon date got pushed back by a couple of hours. Not today, however—today he had *very* special plans. He'd even taken tomorrow off work as well.

'I have a particular surprise. Only *you're* keeping us waiting...' He waggled his brows at her lasciviously.

'Okay.' She chuckled and put her pencil down.

'You've convinced me.' She glanced up at him again with a gleam in her eye. 'You've always been good at that.'

He stepped closer to see the picture she'd been working on. It was miniature perfection. His wife? *Total* perfection. Her cheeks were flushed and there was a smudge of charcoal by her chin and her hair was in the messiest ponytail he'd ever seen. She wore loose linen shorts and a plain, not-quite-white-any-more tee and she was gorgeous.

'I just need two minutes to get changed.' She stood and stretched.

'I'll go see the twins.'

He walked back inside and followed the sound of toddler laughter.

'Daddy!' The stereo call would never get old.

Gracie and Millie ran and clutched a leg each. His soaring heart now swelled to bursting point. They were such delights. He dropped to the ground and they squealed with laughter as he pulled them into a hug and quizzed them on their day.

'How many times did you go down the slide?'

Rosanna skipped to the bathroom and took the quickest ever shower. Time had slipped from her completely. Her parents had taken the girls to the park for an adventure an hour ago and she'd got lost in the garden on the terrace, inspired to do a drawing for her new collection. She'd finally figured out the job of her dreams. Her boss at the nursery up in Brisbane had seen her notebook and loved her botanical sketches. Together they'd designed a limited stationery range to be sold onsite. To

Rosanna's amazement it had taken off and since then she'd expanded her sales online. She was still growing her own plants and now she put together terrariums on request for the store to sell as well. Now her little business was literally thriving.

What was more, her relationship with her parents had improved hugely over the last couple of years. While they had gone to Queensland, once there they'd soon decided to retire. It had completely shocked Rosanna, but they were working on their golf handicaps, of all things. They'd actually relaxed and seemed *happy* with each other. They stayed with Leo and Rosanna quite often— helping out with babysitting when they needed it, loving simple trips to the park and time with their granddaughters. Doing the things they'd not taken the time from work to do with Rosanna when she was young.

Rosanna pulled on a silk slip dress in sky blue and slid her feet into summery sandals. Thursday afternoons were their special dates, but Leo had told her that tonight was an extra-special one and she was to pack an overnight bag. She smiled to herself as she fixed her hair. With Leo, they could be going anywhere.

She went to the twins' bedroom and found him on the floor. He was lying on his stomach reading a story to the girls, who were leaning against him like two little puppies. Her heart melted at the sight.

'Ready?' she asked with a teasing lilt.

'Two minutes.'

She chuckled delightedly. That he took time for them was the greatest sign of his love.

She went to the kitchen where her parents were pottering about making an early pasta dinner. 'Thank you so much.'

'No problem.' Her mother had actually spilled pasta sauce on her shirt.

She shook her head as she passed Axel in his tank and went back to kiss the children.

Leo had finished and rose to meet her. He held her hand as they went down in the elevator and got into the car. It was only a few minutes' drive till they parked up outside his usual helicopter service.

'Well?' She glanced at him. 'When are you going to tell me where we're going?'

'When we get there.'

It was a forty-minute flight, heading north. Not in the direction of her old university, but the wine region. They circled over an estate—from above she admired the large mansion and perfect-looking pool. A few minutes later they'd landed.

'I thought we needed a weekend house.' He glanced at her as they walked across the lawn. 'In the country.'

'A what?'

'A country house.'

Her heart pounded. 'Really? As in to keep?'

'As in, yes.' He took her hand and walked around the outside of the house.

'Are we not going in?'

'There's something at the back I want you to see first.' He smiled at her. 'Back when we met, you couldn't afford a glasshouse so I thought you might like one now.'

Rosanna stopped and stared at what had just come into view. At the rear of the house was another lawn and the focal point? A stunning Victorian-style glasshouse that wouldn't look out of place in a city's botanical gardens. White-painted frames, glass, wrought-iron decorations… Her jaw dropped.

'Leo, it's *magical.*'

'Do you mind that I went ahead and bought it without talking to you first?' He smiled at her. 'Because if you don't like it, we can sell it.'

'Don't you dare.' She nudged him playfully.

'I knew you didn't need to see the actual house.' He laughed. 'I knew this would be enough to convince you.' He pulled out a large iron key from his pocket as they walked towards the greenhouse. 'You have to admit it's romantic.'

He unlocked the door and ushered her in.

Romantic wasn't the word. 'Leo…' Again she stared in awe.

'It got shifted here and I had it restored.' He stepped behind her and wrapped his arms around her waist.

She craned her neck to look at him. 'How long have you been planning this?'

His lopsided smile widened.

The glasshouse wasn't filled with plants yet—she knew he'd left the joy of that for her. But there was a set-up in the corner. Silk screens, behind which? A huge bed with soft-looking linen, a velvety sofa, a small table upon which there was a hamper. She already knew it would be filled with her favourite things. They weren't staying in the house tonight, they were staying here— in paradise.

'This is so perfect.' It was gorgeously lush and indulgent.

'Happy anniversary,' he said, cradling her close.

'But I don't have my gift for you with me.' She leaned back against him.

'I know, I'm early. Couldn't wait any longer.'

It wasn't their anniversary for another three days.

'How can I compete?' She shook her head. 'What can I possibly give you that will match this?'

'You've already given me everything.' He spun her in his arms and gazed into her eyes. 'There's nothing more I could ever want in life other than more time with you.'

Her heart melted because he had warmed up so wonderfully. He was incredible—so determined, so loyal, and all she could do was tell him and show him how much he mattered to her. That, she knew, was everything—because it was what he did for her.

So she smiled and rose on tiptoe to kiss him. 'Time to do this?'

'Please. Lots. Always.'

Direct, honest…with that edge of desperation. She knew there was a last little hunger—a need in him that might always need to be soothed. With laughter. With love. With gentle humour and fierce touch. With the certainty that they *both* needed. Because she was the same. But she was here for him as he was for her. And they'd get there—they already had.

'Mmm…' She teased a thoughtful pose before pressing against him with all her passion and playfulness and underlying truth. 'Then, okay, we have a deal.'

He laughed and she melted at the love shining in his eyes. 'I like doing deals with you best of all.'

* * * * *

WE HOPE YOU ENJOYED
THIS BOOK FROM

HARLEQUIN

PRESENTS

Escape to exotic locations where passion knows no bounds.

Welcome to the glamorous lives of royals and billionaires, where passion knows no bounds. Be swept into a world of luxury, wealth and exotic locations.

8 NEW BOOKS AVAILABLE EVERY MONTH!

#3929 MARRIED FOR ONE REASON ONLY
The Secret Sisters
by Dani Collins
A few stolen hours with billionaire Vijay leaves Oriel with a life-changing surprise—a baby! He demands marriage...but can she really accept his proposal when all they've shared is one—albeit extraordinary—encounter?

#3930 THE SECRET BEHIND THE GREEK'S RETURN
Billion-Dollar Mediterranean Brides
by Michelle Smart
When tycoon Nikos emerges from being undercover from his enemies, he discovers he's a father. He vows to claim his son. Which means stopping Marisa's business-deal marriage and reminding her of *their* electrifying connection.

#3931 A BRIDE FOR THE LOST KING
The Heirs of Liri
by Maisey Yates
After years presumed dead, Lazarus must claim the throne he's been denied. But to enact his royal revenge, he needs a temporary fiancée. His right-hand woman, Agnes, is perfect, but her innocence could be his downfall...

#3932 CLAIMING HIS CINDERELLA SECRETARY
Secrets of the Stowe Family
by Cathy Williams
Tycoon James prides himself on never losing control. It's what keeps his tech empire growing. As does having his shy secretary, Ellie, at his side. So their seven nights of red-hot abandon shouldn't change anything...until they change *everything*!

#3933 THE ITALIAN'S DOORSTEP SURPRISE
by Jennie Lucas

When a mesmerizing and heavily pregnant woman arrives on his doorstep, Italian CEO Nico is intrigued. He doesn't know her name but can't shake the feeling they've met before...and then she announces that the child she's carrying is his!

#3934 FROM ONE NIGHT TO DESERT QUEEN
The Diamond Inheritance
by Pippa Roscoe

Star awakens a curiosity in Sheikh Khalif that he hasn't felt since a tragic accident made him heir to the throne. But surrendering to their attraction is risky when duty decrees he choose country over their chemistry...

#3935 THE FLAW IN HIS RED-HOT REVENGE
Hot Summer Nights with a Billionaire
by Abby Green

Zachary hasn't forgotten Ashling's unparalleled beauty—or the way she almost ruined his career ambitions! But when chance brings her back into his world, Zach discovers he wants something far more pleasurable than payback...

#3936 OFF-LIMITS TO THE CROWN PRINCE
by Kali Anthony

When Crown Prince Alessio commissions his portrait, he's instantly enchanted by innocent artist Hannah. She's far from the perfect princess his position demands. But their dangerous desire will make resisting temptation impossible...

YOU CAN FIND MORE INFORMATION ON UPCOMING HARLEQUIN TITLES, FREE EXCERPTS AND MORE AT HARLEQUIN.COM.

HPCNMRB0721